THESE VIOLENT DELIGHTS

JESSICA RANEY

THIRD WHEEL PUBLISHING

The sword was stuck halfway through its neck. I was beat after taking out nine shamblers and five runners, and maybe my arms didn't have it in them to take the head clean off, but then again, it could have been the blade. Nineteen sticks and the fact that the steel hadn't been that great to start with made it likely that the sword would get stuck in a vertebra on the twentieth swing. Either way, the outcome was the same. The zed was still thrashing around and grabbing for me. Just cutting off their heads halfway didn't do much except rile them up. It needed to come all the way off. The mob was laughing. I guess it was funny to see the blade poking out and the zed grabbing for me with her head drooping to one side and flopping around. Why pay to see clean kills? There wasn't much danger or entertainment value in that, so that's why when they gave us blades, they gave us shitty blades. The mob wanted the bloodshed, but they wanted entertaining bloodshed. Clean kills and easy match-ups didn't bring in money, and since the League was all about the money, we got dull blades or no blades at all. I'd opened up the chest in the middle of the ring to find all sorts of junk in there you wouldn't think you could use to dispatch zeds: an old table leg, a tennis racquet, a glass bottle, a chain. Once I'd even gotten an old fountain pen. That was a hell of a moment, let me tell you, to look down and see nothing but a pen between you and infection, but somehow I managed to kill the three shamblers they'd sent into the arena. My brother Danny always said, "Where there's a will there's a way". I'd seen him get us out of all sorts of scrapes and bad situations with no weapons or supplies, so I knew what was possible. To Danny, no problem was insolvable; he taught me that early on. If you didn't want to be eaten, you'd better find a way with whatever you found in the box. I always found a way.

On this day there happened to be a shitty sword in the box. That was not a surprise because my match was a big one. Fifteen zeds—five of them runners—was a lot. Ten shamblers all at once was a lot too, but you add in those runners, screaming, desperate to tear you to pieces and it would have been nearly impossible to survive unless you had a blade. The League rule was that if your odds were worse than 5:1, you got a blade of some kind. Even the criminals they tossed into the mix got a blade, although it was usually a total piece of junk, but even they got a fighting chance. I wasn't a criminal, but my odds were bad, so I got a blade.

I gave it a tug, but it was stuck in her neck. Sometimes blades did that, got caught in between those neck bones. I needed to get her down on the ground for better leverage if I was going to get it out. I was just about to take her down when I heard a familiar clang. At that same time, the mob went nuts. I whirled and saw the gate to the zed pen open. A runner burst out of the shadows, growling and sprinting toward me. I had agreed to the 15:1, not 16:1. This was a move designed to freak me out or take me out.

The zed wasn't very big, maybe 120 pounds, and he was just a kid, fifteen, or so, but he was fast and he was enraged, likely because they had baited him in the holding pen. I didn't have time to get the sword unstuck from the shambler, so I shoved her backward and out of the way. I turned to focus on the runner.

I was good, but honestly, without that blade, I was kind of in trouble. His brain had to be destroyed somehow or else he would just keep coming until he was dead, a few minutes later, he would start up again. There wasn't anything lying around I could use, but I knew I didn't want to die, so I had to figure it out. Runners were so full of rage that it made them extra strong and fast. Even the ones that had been fat and slow before they were infected somehow got much faster and stronger after; but though they were stronger and faster, they weren't smarter. They didn't think, didn't plan, and they showed absolutely no self-preservation. They ran at you in a berserker rage. I used that to my advantage. I calmed myself and stood perfectly still as he came barreling toward me. Just as he was about to grab me, I sidestepped and tripped him. He went sprawling headlong onto the sand, and before he could get up, I jumped on the middle of his back and pinned him down. I maneuvered until I had his arms tucked under my knees. He howled and thrashed, but I kept his left arm pinned with my leg and pulled his right arm up and back as hard as I could until I felt his shoulder snap. He screamed and thrashed even harder, almost unseating me, but I managed to keep him down. I grabbed his left arm and yanked it until it broke too.

People said that the zeds didn't feel pain, but that wasn't true. The shamblers, maybe not, because they were already dead, but the runners, oh yes, they felt pain. You could see it in their eyes. The pain overwhelmed an actual person, but with zeds, it just enraged them. The second broken arm made him buck wildly, and I went flying off his back. He was on his feet then, his broken arms hanging at odd angles, and he was half sobbing, half screaming in pain and rage as he flung himself on top of me. He couldn't grab me or I would have been done for, but he bit and lunged at me for all he was worth. I managed to get my knees up between us and I kicked, sending him onto his back. The mob was in a frenzy as vicious and as hungry as the zed. They thought they were seeing the end of me for sure, but as soon as he was off me, I was up and on top of him. He was growling and spitting and he had shit himself; he was so mad. I was able to hold him down but my arms were shaking from the effort of keeping him pinned. I knew that I couldn't hold out much longer. I really needed that sword.

He strained upward as I held him, and he let out a noise that you would swear could not have come from a human being. It was a noise so full of hatred and rage and pain that you would hope that no person could have ever had cause to make it. It should have made me recoil. But it didn't. I let the full inhuman blast of that noise and the stink of his rotten breath hit me square in the face and I just stared at him as the mob screamed along with him. I looked into his eyes for a few seconds longer and the crowd hushed, waiting for one of us to do something.

Looking back, I don't know why I did what I did. Maybe it was an unconscious act of showmanship, or maybe I was just pissed and tired of them and their stinking screams, but I waited just a few seconds after he'd finished, then I screamed my own inhuman scream right back into his face. The mob loved it. They exploded in a deafening roar, rattled the chain- link fences, and pounded on the Plexiglas that surrounded the arena. The noise seemed to disorient the zed for just a second, and he went slack. I balled up a fist and flattened his nose. He howled as his nose exploded. I clapped my palms against his ears as hard as I could. Infected or not that hurts like hell. He was totally disoriented, and that was my chance. I jumped up and ran for the shambler with the dangling head. She was up and milling around, so I kicked her legs out from under her. Once she was down, I yanked the blade free from her neck. A quick whack and her head popped right off her body. She was done. The crowd began chanting my name then because they knew the fight was at an end. I had my blade.

The runner had finally shaken off the ear pop and locked on to me. He screamed and charged me again. I planted my legs, angled the blade up, and jammed it up under his ribcage as he crashed into me. His momentum provided all the force I needed.

When runners die for the first time, you can see the humanity return to them. He looked down at the blade, then at me, and he seemed to realize what happened to him. He made a mewing sound, like a kitten, like he was trying to say something but couldn't. In that moment, as they realized what they had become and what was going to happen next, you could almost feel sorry for them.

I got a good look at him. He had a bite mark on his neck, a fresh bite mark without much pus or black streaks that always radiated out from the wound. That meant he was recently infected, as in a few hours ago. They were spryer then, in the first day or so after infection—faster, more rage-filled and much more dangerous. His neck wasn't torn up, like it would have been if his bite had been some kind of accident. This kid was infected on purpose.

As we stood there, in the middle of the arena, listening to the mob scream and chant for me to finish it, I realized that this boy had been infected and tossed in as a twist, a gambit by the people in charge to make things more interesting and sell more tickets. I meant nothing; my life meant nothing. If the kid had bitten me, the show would have gone on. They probably would have sold more tickets than ever for the match, the one where somebody took me out with whatever they pulled out of the chest. The crowd would have cheered just as loud to see me beheaded with a lawnmower blade as they did when I took out the zeds with nothing but a fountain pen. I don't know why any of this had never occurred to me before. Maybe I had always been juiced from the rush, I really don't know, but right then, when all the information, the noise, and the stink hit me, it made me hate everything that I did, everyone that watched, and even myself. I just wanted to be done with it.

He grabbed at my shirt weakly and started to cry. As gently as I could, I pulled the blade free, and he fell onto his back. He was on the sand, spitting blood and bleeding out fast, making those scared kitten sounds and mumbling. He would be dead in a less than a minute but I didn't wait that long. I knelt down beside him. I wanted to say something to him—something reassuring, something nice—but I just really didn't know what to say so I jammed the point of the sword straight down through his eye, twisting the blade to ensure that his first death was also his last death.

The mob roared and chanted my name even louder. Most of the time, I would stand there and smile, letting them all get a good look after I ended a match. My manager said it was good showmanship and a little cockiness was good for my image, but today, I didn't have the stomach for it. I was tired, and sometimes it made me sick, this thing I did. I yanked the blade out of the kid's skull and flung it across the arena where it smacked the glass and left a big red smudge as I stalked out of the ring. That only seemed to make them cheer louder.

2

One thing that had always bothered me about Clay was that he never looked at my body as they decontaminated me. It didn't seem human. I mean, I had to stand there, completely naked as they rinsed me off and checked for bites, scratches, and open wounds, but he was all business. It's not as if I cared exactly that I seemed to have no effect on him. It wasn't ego. It was just unsettling.

"Come on, kid," he said as he sat there counting tickets. "Be reasonable. A few surprises keep it fresh. People love that, and you couldn't have faked that look on your face if you'd known. They ate it up."

"I don't care. No more extra zeds, Clay. That one almost got me," I said as I winced and gave the handler a dirty look as she switched over to bleach water for the final rinse.

Clay laughed. "It wasn't even close. You took him out in less than a minute."

"Yeah, well, how about we throw you in a pit with a fresh runner and see how close you think it is. I won't do it again." The handler finished with the bleach and started drying me off. I scowled at her and took the towel away. "I'll do it myself, thanks."

"Oh yeah, you won't do it again? Not even if I add in an extra ten percent?" He leaned back in his chair and stared at me with a smug look on his face. Ten percent was a lot. That meant he'd made a whole lot more than he thought he would.

"Ten percent? Are you crazy? My life is worth more than a measly ten. With my record and rep, I know you made bank on that. I want twenty-five." I smiled at the way he narrowed his eyes as I threw the towel down and started getting dressed.

"Twenty percent, but I won't guarantee a blade in the box," he said.

I shook my head. "You can't do that. The League has rules. You can't violate the terms of the contract."

He smiled. "I can if I slide the League an extra five. They already said yes to it. Any match outside the odds is eligible so long as the fighter agrees." He was smiling as he straightened his bow tie. "It's your own fault, really,

Em. You make it look too easy. The mob is getting bored. I billed that last one as a no- rules match and I tripled sales."

"I took out sixteen zeds—six of them fresh runners—with a dull, rusty blade. Anyone who thinks that's too easy can come give it a go and see how they fare," I said. I walked over and towered over him as he sat there. "That includes you."

He didn't move. He just smiled. "With an extra twenty, you could move your family into the Third Circle."

I wanted to punch him for that. He had no business bringing them up and reminding me of what I was so very aware of. "Twenty-five. No rules. That's it. Other-wise take this whole deal and shove it right up your ass."

He grinned wider, and I knew then he'd gotten exactly what he wanted. "Deal. And because I love you kid, I'm going to personally set your family up tomorrow."

"Yeah, you're a great guy Clay. The best. At my funeral, make sure you say something nice," I said as we started to walk back through the tunnels to my dormitory.

He laughed and put his arm around me. "Nah, I'll be gone long before you. You know what they're saying about you? They're saying you can't die. And after that match today, that creepy scream thing you did? I'm inclined to believe it."

I shook my head. "That's nuts. I can die just as easily as the next idiot."

"No, kid, you really can't. You do the impossible out there; you always have. That's why I pay you so well. A hundred times, I thought you were done for, yet you always find a way. Death is your talent."

"Gee, thanks," I said as I reached the guarded gate leading to the dormitory. "What an extraordinary talent."

He winked at me. "It is in this place, kid," We stopped. "Your family wants to see you."

I grabbed his shirt and shoved him against the wall. "I told you I don't want them here Clay."

He didn't struggle. "I know, but your brother insisted. They're waiting in the meeting room."

I let him go. "Part of the new deal. They are not ever allowed to see the matches again."

"I can't promise that, Em."

"You can, and you will, or I'm out."

He nodded. "I'll do what I can."

A guard opened the gate to let me through. "Make sure you do. I know you'd hate to lose that much money," I said. I walked through the gate and down the hall toward the meeting room. The guard trailed me the whole way.

"You're only supposed to get thirty minutes, but I won't keep time," the officer said quietly so nobody else could hear. He had a star-struck look in his eye and grinned at me.

I nodded and smiled back at him politely. He was new. Sometimes the new ones had crushes. "Thanks, ah..." I looked for his nametag. "Officer Vance. I really appreciate that, but I won't be long." I smiled at him again and he blushed.

As soon as I entered the room, a tiny body crashed into me and almost knocked me off my feet. My sister Sara was seven, although she looked like a four-year-old she was so small, but she could still pack a wallop. I laughed and picked her up. She wrapped her legs around my waist and nearly choked me with a hug. "Easy Stretch. You'll kill me."

"No way," she said. "You're super tough. Everyone says so."

I gave her a squeeze then shifted her weight onto my hip. She was so skinny that I could feel every rib and see every vertebra. Inside the Second Circle, the security was better and the threat of an outbreak less, but food was still scarce. She had more to eat than most— my winnings made sure of that—but she was still going hungry. "They do, huh? Well I guess opinions on that might vary." I tickled her. "I think you've grown about a foot." I kept tickling her and looked over at my brother Charlie. He was looking at me but not smiling. He knew I had noticed how skinny Sara was, and he knew I blamed him.

"That was a crazy match today. Sixteen?" He shifted his weight around and looked uncomfortable, partly because his shitty prosthetic leg was not fitted correctly, and partly because he knew any attempt to tell me what to do was not going to go over well.

"I gotta do what I gotta do Charlie."

"Sixteen is suicide, Em."

"No, it's rent money," I said. I turned Sara upside down and began to shake her. She giggled and squirmed. "You got any better ideas on how not to starve?" He couldn't farm, couldn't fight, and he couldn't scavenge, not with his leg.

"I've been doing better with the shop." He did a few odd repairs on things, but he was slow and had never had the mechanical abilities that our dad and brother Danny had possessed. Charlie was nothing like Danny, actually. He was mediocre or worse at everything where Danny had been gifted. Danny taught me everything I knew about foraging and science. He made sure I could fight and take care of myself. Charlie made sure I'd always had to work my ass off to keep us all alive.

"The shop isn't enough to feed you, let alone all three of us. Look, Charlie, this is the only way. We can't go back to scavenging." I looked down at Sara, then at him.

Outside the walls was no place for a six-year-old. I had been a six-year-old out there and I knew.

Sara piped up. "We could. I can help."

"No way, Stretch. Out in the Zone is bad news."

She crawled around in my lap and snuggled into my shoulder. "I can handle it. I'm a good fighter, like you. This morning Jacob Kasen told me he hoped you got eaten today, and I broke his nose."

"What have I told you about worrying about what people say about me?" I tilted her face up, and she gave me a sweet, innocent look with her big brown eyes.

"You said to not listen, but Em, Jacob won't shut up. Besides, he hit Max, the kid with one hand that lives down the Row, and I didn't like that, so I busted his nose."

"No fighting," I said as I tapped her upturned nose. I knew she wouldn't listen. I never listened to Danny when he told me not to fight, either. Look where it had gotten me. I was proud of her for being tough. That would keep her alive, but I didn't want her on the path that I was on. I wanted better for her. "I don't care what he does or what he says. You steer clear of him."

She shrugged and nodded. "Okay, I'll try."

I laughed and hugged her again. She would fight the kid the next day if she had to; I would do the same. I looked over at Charlie and my smile disappeared. "I don't want you coming to see the fights anymore."

Charlie shook his head. "You don't tell me what to do. We need to be here in case you need—"

"Need what? Your help?" I looked down at his leg and scoffed. He had always sucked at scavenging and fighting, anyway. A hundred times Danny had saved his ass and a hundred more times I had too. Charlie could help himself least of all. "I don't want Sara seeing all that stuff. I told Clay you couldn't come any more."

"You think you hold all the strings, don't you? You think what you say goes because you earn all the money and you're some hotshot fighter?"

"Yeah, I am a hotshot fighter and I do earn all the money. Somebody has to because you sure as hell won't do it. If we counted on you we'd all be living in a tent in the First Circle still and I'd still be fighting, but not under such good conditions."

"Like I can help this?" he yelled as he pointed to his leg. "You think I want to be dependent on my little sister? You think I want any of this?"

Sara had grabbed my shirt and started to cry. "Don't fight! Please Em, don't."

I hugged her. "It's fine, Stretch. We're not fighting. Hey. Don't cry." I used my shirt to dry her tears. "I don't want you guys coming anymore. Please." I looked over her head at Charlie. "Look, I made a new deal today. You guys are moving to the Third Circle." I ruffled Sara's hair. "And somebody can go to school."

Charlie shook his head. "No. No way."

"It's done, Charlie. You saw what happened today?" He nodded at me. "Well it was going to keep happening. Now at least I'll be getting paid better. Clay is going to take care of getting you guys all set up tomorrow, but please, Charlie, don't come any more."

We looked at each other and he understood. "Okay," he said, "but when your contract is up, you're out. No more, Em."

I nodded. I had already decided that. If I made it through the term, I was out. "Agreed. Look, I gotta get back and you two have to pack." I hugged Sara, and she started to sniffle again. "Look, none of that. You guys are going to have a great new place. I'm gonna get a pass to come see it as soon I can." She looked up at me with the teary eyes. "You promise?"

"I promise," I nodded as I hugged her tight. "Alright, I gotta go." I grabbed Charlie in a one-armed hug. "Everything is going to be fine Charlie."

"If you say so, Em. Just be careful."

"Careful is my middle name," I said.

"No, it isn't. It's—"

I flipped him off as I headed out of the room and back to the dormitory. He was right. It wasn't.

3

I had just finished running my laps for the morning when they brought the new crop of fighters in. They did that every Monday morning after a Sunday fight card. Some of them—most of them actually —would be fighting this coming Sunday, which meant that I would be fighting some of them the Sunday after. I tried to ignore them that first week. There was no sense in making friends only to decapitate them a week later.

They always herded them into the middle of the arena when we were training. I'm not sure why, I mean, I guess they were trying to give them a sense of what it was going to feel like to walk into the arena for their first fight, but having gone through it I can safely say they failed epically to prepare you for what that's like. The new group of fighters was pretty much the same assortment that usually showed up on Mondays. There were a couple fit looking kids, volunteers. They were young and cocky looking. Those ones were always the first to die. If you were that fit that meant you came from the upper Circles and you had no idea how to deal with zeds. They were goners in that first week.

There were three skinny, dirty kids. Their hollow cheeks and layers of grime told me they were used to starving and fighting for any scrap that would help them survive another day. That's what I looked like when I had marched into the arena for the first time. I hadn't eaten in a week and I couldn't even tell you the last time I had taken a real bath. We lived in the First Circle then. I gave the signing bonus to Charlie, and he bought two passes— one for him, and one for Sara, and they moved into the Second Circle that afternoon. They still had to sleep on the streets for a couple of weeks until I won enough to get them a room to rent, but at least it was safer than the First Circle. I was sure these three had similar stories. They would make it at least a week. This was a million times better than what they were used to.

The bulk of the group was convicts. About half the Fighters were criminals. It was a win-win situation for the League. The criminals were good at killing, so the fights were interesting, or they weren't good at killing and it was a guilt-free capital punishment program. Of course that made life interesting for the rest of us because the cons didn't live separately—we had to deal with them—but they had never been a problem for me. I dealt with them in the First Circle for a long time. They would all gravitate toward one another and to a leader and they would survive or not, usually because they sold each other out. Even in the Arena, resources were limited.

I looked over at the current leader of the cons, Rilla. She and her toadies were laughing and pointing at the newbies. Rilla wasn't huge, but she was a decent fighter, at least against Zeds. Against people, she was mean and sneaky, the kind of asshole that would hit you from behind with a chair. I never found out what she did, but she seemed to enjoy violence. She strutted around the dorms and bullied most of the other girls, taking anything they had of value, which was never much, or stealing their food. She and I had come to an understanding when I arrived. By an understanding, I mean I broke her arm when she tried to take my first meal. She definitely hated me after that, and I had to watch my back until I had a good enough rep that she left me alone. We had occasional scraps because she was an asshole and I'm stubborn, but the gist is she left me the hell alone and I didn't interfere with her lording around the dorms. I didn't really care. I mean, if somebody wasn't strong enough to stand up to her or smart enough to kiss her ass they sure didn't stand much chance in the arena, so I had no use for them.

Anyway, Rilla was looking over the newbies, especially the cons, and I knew she was looking for anyone who stood out as a threat to her, or for new girls to torture. Rilla nudged her main toady, Mya—a tall, skinny, blonde girl who was mean as a snake and dumb as a box of rocks—and I looked toward where they pointing. Their target was a short brunette with big glasses that she kept pushing up on her nose. She wore clean clothes, and looked delicate and pale, like she didn't go out in the sun much. She looked like higher Circle to me—the clothes alone screamed at least Fourth Circle—but then I saw the handcuffs and I realized she was a con. Whatever she did must have been bad because she came from money and that should have been enough for her to buy her way out. The fact that it hadn't spoke volumes. The girl looked terrified as the League official explained the rules and schedule to them. She bit her lip and pushed her glasses up nervously as she shifted from foot to foot. She was doing it so much she looked like she was shaking. If she was smart, she should have been shaking because her nervous ticks drew even more attention to her. Rilla and her crew were laughing aloud at her. I just shook my head and started running again. I didn't need to stand around and hear any more.

I stayed and ran well past the time anyone else was training, and by the time I got back inside, everyone else had gone through showers and were sitting down to eat the mid-day meal. I had just gotten my food and sat down at my table to eat when the guards ushered in the newbies. The groups I had predicted had formed up. The new volunteers with each other, and the Cons formed up too, all except the pale girl with the glasses. She walked through with her tray and passed up each table due to the dirty looks she was getting from everyone. She finally found an empty table next to mine, sat down, and looked at her food. The look on her face confirmed to me that she was Upper Circle because she wrinkled her nose at the stew and poked through it with her spoon. As far as food went, it wasn't the best, but there was plenty of it and you got it regularly, which was a new thing for all the fighters from the Lower Circles. I remember the day I first came in. I hadn't eaten in a week, and the stew they gave me that first day tasted so good that I slurped it down in about five seconds and ate another bowl just as fast. It didn't matter that I couldn't identify the meat. The new girl, however, was clearly not used to starving because she had no interest in eating it. She put her spoon down as she shook her head, then picked up her hunk of bread and began to eat it delicately. I rolled my eyes and went back to my own food. She wouldn't last the week.

Rilla was holding court at her usual table on the other

side of the room. The new cons had formed up over there around her and they were all chattering and cursing at each other, jockeying for position in the pack. Rilla seemed content with all of it until she saw the pale girl sitting by herself. She scowled, then smiled, which in my experience with her meant something bad was going to happen. She slapped Mya and her other minion, Jane, on the arms and pointed at the new girl. I couldn't hear what she said to them, but they laughed, then the three of them got up and walked over to the new girl's table. Rilla plopped down, took the bread right out of the girl's hand, and ate it.

"Something wrong with your food?" Rilla asked, her mouth full of bread.

"I'm not very hungry at the moment," the girl said in a clipped, formal accent.

"Oh, really? Well in here, I decide who's hungry and who ain't. I say when you eat and when you don't." Rilla chewed another big bite of bread, then smiled with her mouth full and spit the mouthful into the bowl of stew. She spit once more into the bowl and smiled as she slid it over to the girl. "Right now, I say you eat."

The girl didn't even look at the bowl; she kept her eyes on Rilla. "No thank you. I'm still not hungry."

Mya and Jane moved around behind the girl. Rilla sort of half laughed. "You're missing it. I say you are. Eat it."

The girl pushed her glasses up on her nose—her

nervous gesture—then crossed her arms. "Perhaps the problem is that you don't understand English or possibly you are a little slow witted, I'm still not certain, but I will speak more slowly so that you will understand... I... am... not... hungry."

I laughed. Nobody except me had ever spoken to Rilla that way, and her face was as red as her hair. She blew out a breath and nodded at Mya and Jane. They both bumped into the girl and stood even closer.

"You don't decide nothing in here. I decide everything. Like, I decide how bad I'm gonna fuck you up. Now, you do what I say and I don't fuck you up so bad you become a Zed before your first fight. You don't do what I say and well..." Mya and Jane bumped the girl again.

The girl still had looked everywhere but Rilla's face, which showed more composure that I had thought she had in her. She uncrossed her arms and smiled at Rilla. "Your eloquent logic has moved me. I suddenly find myself famished." She picked up her spoon and held it over the bowl as Mya and Jane laughed behind her and Rilla looked smug. The girl was still smiling when she picked up the bowl and threw its contents into Rilla's face.

Rilla started sputtering and stood up as she wiped the stew and spitball out of her eyes. "You are fucking dead. Hold her."

Mya and Jane grabbed the girl and pulled her up and around the table. Rilla balled up her fist and was about to start pounding the girl when I did something stupid. I got involved.

Talking to Rilla wouldn't have done any good, and I had never been much good at it, anyway. There was only one thing Rilla understood. Before Mya or Jane had even seen me or could warn her, I grabbed Rilla by her red ponytail and slammed her nose into the table. Her face was red with blood and she screamed. Mya and Jane looked shocked, and so did the new girl. All three stared at me with their mouths wide open. I held Rilla's head back as she coughed and spit blood all over.

"Rilla, you're going to leave this girl alone. You get it?" I asked.

"Bitch, I will kill you too," she yelled.

I slammed her face into the table again. Jane and Mya let go of the new girl and came around the table. I shoved Rilla down on the floor and kicked her in her stomach. She lay there moaning and spitting blood. I turned my attention to the two women. Neither one of them was a decent fighter. "Really? You two think that's going to work out for you?" I said as they took a step toward me. They thought better of it and picked Rilla up. I motioned toward the new girl. "Leave this one alone or you will deal with me."

Rilla was totally out of it and covered in blood. Mya

looked down at her then back at me. "She is going to kill you for this."

"Yeah, she said that already. I guess she can try." The new girl still hadn't moved. The other cons were starting to come our way, and that's when the guards got interested. They moved in to assert some control and the cons didn't like it. I knew that was my cue to get out of there. I snapped my fingers at the new girl. "Hey, you, come on. Let's go." She stared at me and I thought she might refuse, but she let out a little puff of air and nodded. I pushed her in front of me roughly and we walked out of the mess hall and down the corridor toward my room.

"My room is the other way," she said. "My things are there."

"No they aren't. Those other cons stole your stuff. You don't have anything anymore. And from now on you stay with me," I said as we reached my room. The rooms were designed to house four people, but I was alone. Being number one was great like that. "Take one of the bunks over there. Stay out of my way and I'll stay out of yours."

"I don't understand."

I flopped down on my bunk and put my hands behind my head. "You won't survive the night if you go back there. They won't come after you in here."

"I understood that part. What I don't understand is why you intervened."

I shrugged. "Me neither." I really didn't. I hated Rilla

and her band of idiots, but I had seen them do that same thing many times. I didn't know why this time was different.

"So you just expect me to live here and do what? Be your possession?" She pushed her glasses up on her nose and crossed her arms as she stared at me.

I laughed at all that, then closed my eyes. "I expect you to leave me alone. I'll make sure nobody messes with you. Unless you annoy me. Then you can go back and be Rilla's. Trust me, you will like that a lot less."

"Oh I have no doubt of that," she said as she sat down on the opposite bunk. "I suppose I should thank you."

"Don't sound so grateful."

She shrugged and pulled her knees up under her. "So I last another few days? I can't do what you do."

She was right. I knew she had never had to fight a zed in her life. When she fought her first match on Sunday, she was probably not going to make it, and it wasn't my problem.

"You'll do what you have to do. Figure it out like the rest of us."

"So you save me and don't care what happens to me?"

I shrugged and nodded. "Yeah. Pretty much."

"I don't believe you," she said. "You jeopardized your safety to help me."

I sat up on my elbows and looked at her. "No I didn't. The guards won't let anything happen to me. And even if that wasn't true, I am still bigger and badder than anybody else in here."

"Really? Then why did you leave the hall? If you are the best, as you claim, why not fight everyone?"

"Because I fight for money. And also, I'm not stupid." She stared at me smugly. "Remember what I said about not annoying me?"

"Do you even care to know my name?"

I reclined back down on my bunk and closed my eyes. "Not particularly."

"It's Claire."

"I don't care."

"Do you want to know why I'm here?" she asked quietly.

"Nope."

"I was framed for a crime."

I laughed. "Ah, ok. Sure. What was it? Did you wear the wrong shoes to some Fifth Circle party?"

"No," she said as she stretched out on her bunk. "They framed me because I discovered a way to cure the infected."

I sat up and looked over at her. "Oh, okay, so you're just a general, all-around batshit kind of crazy. Cool. Please be quietly crazy." I reclined and closed my eyes.

"I'm not crazy."

"You are clearly crazy. You made a fuss and picked a fight you couldn't win and you claim to be able to do things that are impossible. Look, I don't care. I'll keep you from bad, weird stuff until the end of the week. After that, you're on your own."

"What if I last longer?" she asked.

"Not my problem," I said.

She looked at me with a look of disbelief mixed with exasperation that I would come to know well. "If you really believed that, you would have let her kill me."

I sighed. "Well, it isn't the first time I did something stupid and it likely won't be the last."

"Let's hope," she said.

4

I finished my last lap then launched into a bunch of pushups and sit-ups. Most everyone else was drilling with weapons, swords, spears and the like. Claire stood at the armory cage, looking at a sword. I watched her pick it up — she could barely lift it. When she swung it, she overbalanced and fell over. All the other fighters saw, and they laughed. Rilla was sitting on a bench; her nose was a complete mess. She stared at Claire and smiled. Everyone knew that Claire was toast on Sunday.

I scoffed at Claire when she told me she knew about a cure for the zeds. That wasn't the absolute most crackpot thing anyone had ever said to me but it was close. Once, a guy in the Male Guild had told me he could talk to the zeds and he was going to turn them into an army in the arena. He really believed it, but as soon as he tried to chat up a shambler, a runner grabbed him and ate his face. I figured Claire was a nut bag too, and like all nut bags that couldn't fight, she would end up a resident of the Dead Pen.

She definitely couldn't fight. She weighed a hundred pounds and her arms had no muscle on them. I suspected she had never lifted anything heavier than a pen in years. She was smart though. As I did my sit-ups, I watched her swing the sword a few more times, then shake her head. She put it down and picked up a spear. That was a better option for her for sure. It would keep the zeds at a decent distance and it was lighter than the sword. She brought the spear over to where I was training and stabbed it into the sand. "Can you show me how to use this?" she asked.

I didn't stop doing my crunches. "See that sharp, pointy end? Stick that in their head."

"That's it? That's all the knowledge you have?"

I finished my set and shrugged. "It's a spear. That's all the knowledge you need."

Claire sighed heavily and leaned on the shaft. "You are the best fighter in the League. There has to be more you can tell me."

I grabbed my towel and wiped my face off. "The length is good. It will keep them away from you. That's what you want. Pin them down and take out the brain. Don't get cute and try to twirl it around and be all fancy."

I pointed over toward one of Rilla's minions, who was yelling and twirling around a spear. "All that's going to do is wear you out. Keep it simple. Stab. Stab. Stab."

"Okay. That's actually intelligent advice," she said as she watched the girl with the spear.

"Thanks. You sound doubtful I had any in me."

"I never really considered that you people thought much. I just thought you-"

"You just thought we were mindless killers? Like the zeds?"

"Worse than them. They can't help it. They're ill."

I felt my face get hot at the insult. "Yeah. They are. Guess what cures them?" I grabbed the spear and threw it at a dummy. It stuck in the head and quivered. "It's really not a good idea to insult us mindless killers."

"I didn't mean to insult you. I was just being honest."

"You think that makes it okay? You can be honest and still be an asshole."

She nodded. "I apologize." She paused and watched me stretch. "You don't train with the weapons. Everyone else does. Why don't you?"

I regarded her for a minute. Nobody had ever asked me why I trained the way that I did. She was definitely smart, even if she was crazy and kind of a dick. The question was why was I telling her the truth? "Because the best way to stay alive in the arena is to be patient. That means avoiding zeds until the right opportunity presents itself."

She smiled at me. It was a genuine one. The first I had seen from her and it was a nice smile. "You run when you train so that you won't get tired during the match. That's very clever."

"Who cares how good you are with a blade? I mean, don't get me wrong, you have to handle one correctly, but you're not fighting another person. The zeds can't think. They don't have skills. You don't need to parry and thrust. You need to last long enough to stab them in the fucking brain when you get the chance. If you're worn out? Well…"

She nodded. "I understand. So I should be running?"

I shrugged. "Do whatever you want. You fight Sunday. You're not going to get fit in four days. You're not going to get strong enough to swing a blade in four days."

"I'm asking you what I should do," she said as she put her hands on her hips. I could see fear and frustration on her face. The truth was, she was screwed. She couldn't fight, and she wasn't strong enough to power her way through it like most of the other Cons.

"Honestly, what you should do is eat well, rest, stay calm, and don't over think it. You'll probably pull a blade in the box."

She picked up the sword and tried to hold it but she

was straining. "That won't do me much good. I can barely hold it."

"Oh you won't get one of these." I took it from her. "You will get a machete or a Bowie knife. Something smaller. That's good for you. You should hope for a kitchen knife."

"I don't think I could use one of those, either." She shook her head and sat down in the sand.

I grabbed her by her shirtfront and hauled her up. "Look, if you want to live, you better figure out how to use one. You must want to because you've been bothering me all day about it, so learn, or shut up and stop wasting my time."

She nodded. "Okay," she said quietly. "Show me."

I spent the next couple of hours showing her some tactics and how to handle a few small blades, ones that she was likely to find in the box when it opened. She was awful, but she tried. When we were finished, she was exhausted. I was sure she had never done as much physical exercise in her entire life as she had in those few hours. That night, she went right to sleep as soon as she hit her rack. For the next few days, we did the same thing —trained and rested. At the end of those four days, she still sucked. Yeah, she still sucked a lot, but before she had a five percent chance of surviving her fight. After the four days, she had a solid twenty percent chance.

That Sunday, she was the last match. The new volunteers had both been bitten. Rilla's new minions scraped by, but they were alive. They were triumphant and cocky as they sat in the Fighter's Box, right outside the gate. I heard them laughing and cat calling to Claire. Everyone had bet against her, and they couldn't wait to see her torn apart. "Okay," I said as we waited for the gate to open. "You walk out to the middle and open the box. Whatever it is, just stay calm. It will probably be a blade. Avoid the shamblers. Focus on the runner. There's only going to be one. Just stay calm."

She nodded. "You said that already."

"Yeah, well, it's the main thing." This was probably going to be the last time I saw her. Well, maybe not. I could be seeing her in my next match, right before I chopped off her head. It didn't help anyone to think about that. "Good luck."

She held out her hand. "Thank you for all of your help. I appreciate it."

I took her hand and shook it. "You're welcome. You'll be okay."

She shook her head. "I highly doubt it, but if I had any chance, it was due to you."

The door to the arena slid open and the light coming from the open space blinded both of us. She took a deep breath, then exhaled slowly before she stepped out into the light.

"Stay calm," I yelled as I climbed up into the Fighter's

Box. The catcalling stopped when I got into the Box, and everyone scooted down the bench to make room. They gave me a lot of room.

Rilla looked down the bench at me and smirked. "Hope you had a good time with your toy," she said. "I can't wait to be the one to spike her next Sunday."

I smirked back. "I hope you can go next week. That nose won't keep you on the bench but a couple of broken arms will."

The crowd was going crazy, chanting for Claire to open the box. She looked confused and terrified, but I watched her center herself as best she could and walk calmly out into the middle of the arena where the box had been placed. Claire closed her eyes and held her breath as she opened the box.

I didn't realize that I was holding my breath too until she pulled the table leg out of the box. The mob screamed. She was supposed to have a blade. It was the rules, and they knew the rules better than anyone did. I heard Rilla laugh. "Looks like I ain't the only one that hates your girl."

I ignored her and focused on Claire. She looked at the table leg as if she had no idea what to do with it. It wasn't the worst thing she could have pulled, but it wasn't what she was expecting, and she was shaken up. I cupped my hands and yelled to her. "Stay calm. Nothing has changed. Claire! Do you hear me? The plan hasn't changed!" She heard me because she turned in my direction and nodded. The doors to the zed pen opened, and the mob erupted again as I counted eight shamblers. They staggered out of the pen toward Claire. She shook as she gripped the table leg like a baseball bat. Eight shamblers weren't that bad, not really, not if she focused, took them out at the knees, and bashed in their heads. "Knees, then heads," I yelled.

Claire took out the first shambler's knees. It took her a couple of whacks, but she got its head. I could tell that her adrenaline had kicked in and she was doing well; she had taken out three more. At the halfway point, she was showing signs of getting tired. Her arms shook and her breathing was labored. On the sixth shambler, she missed, overbalanced, and fell over. The mob went crazy because they smelled the end. Claire managed to get back up and grab the table leg, but the three remaining zeds caught up to her. Claire retreated carefully, but finally, she was directly below us, backed up against the arena wall. We were all on our feet, looking down at her. She was covered in gore, and when she tried to lift the table leg, she couldn't. It fell to the sand in front of her and she dropped her head, exhausted and defeated. Everyone in the arena knew she was done for. That's when I did yet another dumb thing.

When I vaulted over the side of the wall and into the arena, the mob went insane. It wasn't very high up, maybe ten feet, but as I hit the ground, my ankle rolled and I lost my balance. I was up quickly, but when I tried to put weight on my ankle, pain shot up my leg. The crowd saw me hop on one leg and realized what happened. They screamed even louder, in shock or excitement to see me die, I didn't know. I ignored them, grabbed the first shambler, and threw it into the other two. They all collapsed in a heap and I motioned for Claire to move away from the wall. "Gimme that leg."

She dragged the leg to me, not able to heft it all the way. "Come on, come on," I yelled as I snapped my fingers. I grasped the table leg and tried to stand on both my legs. It wasn't going to happen. I looked over at Claire. She was completely out of breath and her arms were shaking. She looked up at me with wide eyes. She was terrified, but I didn't just see fear there, I saw trust.

The shamblers were up now and moving toward us. I looked down at Claire and handed her back the table leg. "Keep them off my back," I said.

She shook her head. "I-I don't think I can."

"You got no choice, do you hear me?" She shook her head and looked defeated. The zeds were closing in. The noise of my hand hitting her cheek seemed abnormally loud even with all the screaming of the mob. She jumped when I slapped her, but she stopped crying, and her eyes were clear and focused as she brought her hand up to rub her cheek. "Keep them off my back. I'll do the rest."

She nodded and gripped the table leg as she looked down at my ankle. "What are you going to do?" she asked.

"Kill them," I said as I turned and launched myself at the closest zed. I could feel it snapping at me as we hit the ground. I had a better chance off my feet. I maneuvered until I was on top of the zed. It was making the chittering noise they made when they were excited. I pinned its arms down with my knees and shoved my forearm up under its chin to close its mouth. It struggled, but it wasn't fresh and didn't really have enough strength to push me off. I brought my other elbow down and busted its head. It stopped struggling, and I extracted my goo-covered arm from what was left of its head. I scrambled off it and turned around on my hands and knees. Claire was struggling with a second zed. I hoisted myself up on my good leg, and as soon as I got my balance, I launched myself at it. It was a ripe one, too—it didn't take much to kill it. The third one, however, was fresh. It had just had its first death and hadn't had time to rot. No way could I smash its head in without breaking open my skin. It was spry, too, and wasn't easy to subdue. I had to use every ounce of strength I had as I dug my knees into the sand and pressed down with all my weight. I looked up at Claire. She shook as she stared down at me and she dropped the table leg into the sand. "What are you waiting for? Kill it," I yelled, but she just stood there. The thing kicked out and happened to hit my bad ankle squarely. I screamed and lost focus on anything except the pain. That was the opportunity the zed needed to buck me off. It scrambled around in the dirt as it grabbed for me and took hold of my pant leg. I was surprised at how tight its grip was for a zed. I shook my leg but couldn't make it let go. It was just about to take a chunk out of my calf when Claire smashed its head in with the table leg. Her face was white, and the flecks of black and red gore stood in stark contrast with her skin. Her eyes were wide and wild as she looked down at me. Then she held out her hand and helped me stand.

The noise from the mob was deafening as they chanted my name. I grabbed Claire's hand and led her out into the middle. "Come on, we gotta do this." When we got to the center, I paused for a few seconds, then I lifted our linked hands into the air. I flung the table leg at the Plexiglas of the rich section just as I had with my sword. The mob loved it. I let them scream and chant for a while, then turned in a big circle to acknowledge the whole arena. As we turned, I looked up into the League Box and saw that the League Council was filing out of the box quickly. The Commissioner turned as she was leaving. She looked down at me with a strange half smile and gave a little salute. Something about the gesture made the hair on the back of my neck stand on end.

5

Claire cowered in the corner while I stood there with four handlers and a doctor examining me. She had flatly refused to take her clothes off, and because they were more worried about me, they ignored her for the time being. Clay was so angry with me he was shaking and had trouble speaking, which was something foreign to him.

"What the hell were you thinking? You-you could have been infected! For what? A con?" he said as little flecks of spittle collected at the corners of his mouth. His face was red, and when he said "con," he made a face as if he had just eaten something bitter.

I just shrugged and tried to keep the weight off my injured ankle. I was covered in gore and the handlers worked quickly to cut my clothes off so they could hose me down. "I wasn't really thinking," I said.

"Too right! You weren't!" Clay yelled as he slammed his fist down on the table. "You broke every rule of the arena."

I rolled my eyes at him. "Dipshit, there are no rules of the arena. The League proved that when she didn't draw a blade in her box. She should have gotten a blade."

"So the fuck what Emily?" He gestured toward Claire. "She is a fucking criminal slated for execution. The rules don't apply to her."

"Since when?" I asked. They pulled off all of my putrescence soaked clothing and began carefully hosing me off. The water was freezing cold. I jumped a little and accidentally put weight on my bad ankle. I yelped and winced. "Cons get the same odds as the rest of us." They always have before. But her? They fucked her over. Why? I mean look at her. She's totally incompetent, and even with a blade she probably would have been toast."

"I'm standing right here," Claire said dryly.

"Are you even listening to yourself? If she was toast either way, why stick your neck out? You are especially stupid sometimes." Clay sucked in a couple of big breaths as he tried to return himself to his normal calm and controlled state. "Let me break this down for you Emily. The League is pissed. You showed them up and screwed up whatever plan they had for her." He jerked his thumb toward Claire. "That's not good. However, you make them a lot of money so they are going to call you before them for some kind of meeting as a courtesy. That's also not good. And what's *especially* not good is the fact that you fucked up your ankle and you have the biggest match of your career coming up in seven days. You better hope you heal quickly or—"

"Or I die. Guess what? There's a really good shot of that happening no matter what, Clayton." The doctor looked me over for any open wounds. She examined my elbows and arms where I had smashed in the zeds' heads. In hindsight, that wasn't a very smart way to kill them as the risk of opening up my skin on a bone fragment was high. Fortunately, their skulls had been completely rotten and soft, so they had kind of just collapsed. My elbows were bruised but not cut. Satisfied that I wasn't infected, the doctor nodded to the handlers, and they started blasting me again with water and strong lye soap and finally, the bleach rinse. I grabbed the towels from them after they finished and dried myself off. It was tough balancing on one leg but I refused to give Clay the satisfaction of seeing me sit down. "Look Clay, I'm not saying it was one of my more brilliant ideas, okay? However, you need to look at the upside. What's the word from the mob?"

"They loved it, of course," he said as he scowled at me.

"Yeah. And what else? There's buzz about her now too, right?"

He nodded. "Yes. But that's not good."

"Why the hell not? They love drama," I said as I finished drying myself and put new clothes on. I finally sat down in order pull on my pants. I had to stop myself from exhaling and sighing in relief. The ankle was throbbing.

"Because they don't want attention drawn to her. You screwed that up too."

"Eh, they'll get over it when they see attendance sales next week," I said. The doctor swooped in to look at my ankle. I gave her the stink eye and growled at her as she prodded it. It was swollen and turning purple.

"Sprained," she said to Clay as she ignored me all together. These doctors did that, treated us like somebody's pet and not like a human being. Normally I ignored it, but today my patience was short. I grabbed her shirtfront and made her look at me.

"Talk to me, not to him," I said. She stared at me and flushed as she tried to loosen my grip. I smiled at her and let her go.

"It's not a bad sprain, but you need to get some ice on it and rest," she said as she straightened her shirt and backed away from me. "I'll write an order for that to go to your cell."

I shook my head. "No way. Bring it here right now."

Clay nodded at her. "Yeah Doc, let's do all that here." He knew that I couldn't be seen as weak in the Dorms. There were unfriendly eyes and ears there and they didn't need to see that I was hurt badly enough for that.

"Also, you need to bring her a shot of cortisone and some anti-inflammatory medication. Enough for the whole week."

Clay, the doctor, and I turned our heads all at once in the same direction to look at Claire. I had forgotten that she was even there.

"Those are all very expensive items. We don't just give those out to these people," the doctor said.

"She's the League's star. Don't you think they want her healthy for her match?" Claire asked as she folded her arms across her chest and looked over her glasses disapprovingly at the doctor.

"Like they care? They make money either way," the doctor said as she started packing up her kit. I grabbed her and shoved her against the wall.

"Give me whatever she said and give it to me now or you don't walk out of this room," I said in a low and calm voice.

"Em, really," I heard Clay say as he put a hand on my shoulder. I shrugged it off.

"I-I don't have it," she stuttered. I heard Claire come up behind me.

"Do you know what a doctor with two broken arms

and two broken knee caps is called?" Claire asked. "No? Bait. They're called bait." Claire rummaged around in the doctor's bag and pulled out a vial, syringe, and a bottle of pills. She held them up. "These will do."

"You can't- they inventory all of that! I'll get in trouble and so will you," the doctor yelled as she struggled against me. I gave her a hard slap across the face.

"You're already in trouble and so am I," I said. "I'm already in the worst place they can send me. You on the other hand... I can see things getting much, much worse and much, much more painful for you if you don't keep your trap shut about this." I let the doctor down but poked her in the forehead. "If you tell anyone about this, I promise you I will find you."

She held her hand to her cheek and rubbed it. One of the benefits of being famous for killing things was that when you threatened normal people with violence, they tended to believe you. She just nodded and looked like she was going to start crying. I jerked my head toward the door. "Beat it." She grabbed her bag and got out as fast as she could. The handlers were laughing as the door shut behind her. I looked at Clay and nodded to the handlers. "They need taken care of."

He agreed. His natural calm seemed restored, and he was thinking like himself again, which was to say he was thinking shiftily. He spoke quietly to them, and I saw him hand them a nice bit of money. That usually kept them quiet. I looked at Claire. She was standing there, a mess from head to toe. Her clothes were sprayed with black, rotted blood and she had bits of zed on her glasses and in her hair. "You need to take your clothes off so they can decontam you."

She looked at me as if I were speaking Chinese. "I hardly think that's necessary."

I laughed at her. "Uh, well, they don't care what you think is necessary. They will do it no matter if you approve or not."

"I'm not just going to-to take my clothes off here in front of total strangers."

"Oh you will. There are more of them than you and I'm not taking you back to my room like that." I pointed at the handlers, who were laughing at her.

She looked over at them, then at me, then handed me the medical stuff. "Don't look at me," she said as she started taking off her clothes. "You there, guard," she pointed to Vance. "Bring some ice in a bucket of cold water." She looked over at me and pointed to the chair. "Get off that ankle. You have to get the swelling down. Prop it up. When that guard brings back the bucket, put your foot in it for a while."

Vance was red in the face. He wasn't used to being ordered around by a con. However, she was a well-spoken con, and she had an air of authority and confidence natural to those from the higher circles. Vance, like most of the rest of the population, was used to doing what they said. He looked at her, his face contorted in confusion and indecision. I limped over to him and touched his arm as I smiled. "Please Vance? It would sure help me out."

His face turned a deeper shade of red, but not one born of anger. He nodded and gave me a slight smile back. "Okay. I'll be right back with it.

"Thanks. I'll owe you one," I said. He nodded and saluted as he left the room. I looked over at Claire. She finally had all of her clothes off and the other handlers had swooped in on her and were hosing her off. She complained about the cold water as she tried to keep bits of herself covered. I shook my head. "Relax. Nobody cares that you're naked." I gestured to the handlers who had doused her with a bunch of soap and prodded her to scrub herself. "They couldn't care less. I couldn't care less. Clay could definitely not care less." He had been quiet as he studied her, not because she was naked, but because of the way she had behaved with the doctor.

"Looks like all the damage here has been done. I'll let you know when your meeting is going to happen. Try to stay out of trouble until then." He looked over at Claire and scowled as he left the room.

Claire was finally in the drying process and the handlers backed away after they declared her bite free. "Don't give them a hard time. They're just doing their jobs," I said as she sat down next to me and pulled on her new clothes.

"The bleach wasn't necessary," she said as she rubbed her eyes.

"Again, they don't give a fuck what you think is necessary." I waved at them as they left the room. "You had zed blood all over you. They use an abundance of caution. Besides, if you're smart enough to know about this," I said as I held up the medicine, "You're smart enough to know you don't take any chances."

She yanked on her shoes "Well they could have given me a privacy curtain."

"Privacy is a luxury you won't have again." We looked up as Vance came back with the bucket full of ice water. "Thanks Vance."

He nodded. "Yeah, um, I'm going to wait outside Em. Just knock when you're done and I'll take you back to the dorm." He motioned toward my ankle. "You gonna be okay?"

I waved nonchalantly at my swollen ankle. "Whatever man, this is nothing. I'm fine. Be ready to rock on Sunday, no problem. Thanks though." I winked at him. He blushed again and smiled as he nearly fell out the door. I turned my attention to the ice bucket. I wasn't prepared for how painful it was to put my foot in the ice bath. The cold was like fire, a million tiny white-hot fires to be exact, and I hissed as I immersed my foot.

Claire looked down at it and nodded. "I know it hurts. Just keep it in there for fifteen minutes or so then we'll take a look at it." She gave me a couple of the pills. "Take these." She kept her eyes on the ice bath. "Your manager is right. What you did was really stupid."

"You'd be in the Zed Pen right now if I hadn't," I said as I downed the pills.

"Maybe that would have been for the best," she said. "They want me there. You know as well as I do that if they want me there, I'll end up there."

"Not for a while," I said. "You heard the mob. They loved that shit. They love us. You keep their love and The League can't do much."

She laughed and shook her head. "You think they're going to let that stop them? Do you even know anything about these people? No matter how much the masses love us," she gestured back and forth between us, "they aren't going to let me live, and now they may not let you either."

"Oh, yeah, by the way, you're welcome," I said. "Look, let's not get all worked up about this. We'll figure it out when they make a move. It's not like it's a mystery as to what that will be."

"Yes, I mean thank you for saving my life. Again. But Emily, really, I can't let you get hurt for me again."

"You don't let me do anything. I do what I want to do." I poked her in the chest. "I'll take my lumps from The

League. They'll talk a little. I'll listen. Whatever. The fact is that we are in danger every minute of every day, even when a bunch of shadowy rich fucks aren't out to get us. They're the ones who don't get that." I tilted my head at her. "But the one thing we agree on is that they really do want you dead."

She nodded. "Very badly."

6

I didn't have to wait long before the League made their move. By Tuesday, whatever was in the magic shot Claire gave me kicked in and my ankle was feeling better. I still couldn't really run so I was just walking around the arena, testing it out. First thing in the session, I made Claire run a bunch of laps and do a bunch of drills. She wasn't happy about it, but I had to give her credit, she took what I dished out with minimal bitching. She was in shitty shape, but she wasn't dumb, and most importantly, she seemed to want to stay alive, so she listened and did what I told her.

We had just finished doing some calisthenics when Clay showed up. He hated coming into the arena, so I knew what was happening the second I saw him walk through the gate. He had a pinched look on his face and didn't have his normal smarmy swagger as he motioned for me to follow him. Claire looked scared too, and she put a hand on my arm as I turned to leave.

"Look, don't try to protect me. Just promise them whatever they want, okay?"

I shook her hand off and smiled. "Oh, don't worry, I'll throw you under the bus if it comes to that."

She looked confused. "What does that mean?"

"It's an expression my dad used to use. Means I'm not going to protect you. I'm only out for myself."

She gave a little laugh and shook her head. "You should be, but you don't seem to have enough sense. Em, be careful."

I waived her off and walked toward Clay. "Why does everyone keep telling me that?" I refused to limp or give anything away that I wasn't 100% fit. Everybody in the place had eyes on me and Claire since Sunday and word would get out if I had been gimping around, so I gritted my teeth and did my best to walk normally. Clay was fidgety and nervous as we walked up to the gate to the Fourth Circle. He had a pass, and his hand shook as he gave it to the guards. They examined it, nodded at him, and smiled at me as I went through the door. I was sure to make eye contact and smile back. It was important to make them feel like I would remember them. People love the idea of famous people knowing who they are.

I had never been in the Fourth Circle before, and I

had to stop and look around a minute as the gate closed behind me. The first thing you notice about the Fourth Circle is how quiet it is; there's no marketplace, no homeless people, and you can't hear any generators going. I was so used to their hum. The silence and lack of clustered people in the street left me feeling unsettled. The sound of our feet hitting the concrete as we walked was so foreign and unnerving to me that I stopped every few feet just to make sure the sound stopped when I did. The second thing I noticed was how clean it was: no trash, no stray animals, no smell of sweat and dirt. The living spaces all were solid and had doors. They were spaced far apart, and they all had little front patios that the residents had decorated with little flags and plants. It was so bizarre that I stopped and stared. Clay turned and looked at me, annoyed.

"Jesus, Em, will you knock it off? We have an appointment."

"What is all this stuff?" I said as I fingered the fabric of a little flag that had a frog wearing sunglasses sitting in a little boat that said, "Summertime Fun Time."

He shrugged and tugged on my arm. "Decorations. Who cares? Let's go."

"They had to buy this stuff? They have money to buy this stuff?"

"Yeah, they do. And a lot more, now come on. We can't be late."

I shrugged. "We can be, but probably won't. Why don't you just chill?"

"Because, Emily, the League Commissioner has requested a meeting. Do you know anyone who has met with her?" He looked at me and raised his eyebrows as I stayed quiet. "Yes. Exactly, nobody. It's kind of a big deal, so can we please go?"

I followed him all the way through the Fourth Circle. It wasn't as big as I thought it would be, and even though I was walking slowly, I found myself staring at the heavy metal gate to the Fifth Circle within ten minutes. The huge gate was plate steel and guarded by five guys with big automatic weapons. It had been a long time since I had seen those kinds of guns. We found a cache of them once on a scavenging trip and I wanted to keep one, but my brother Danny said they were more of a pain in the ass than they were worth, so we sold them. These people were serious business— their facial expressions never changed as Clay handed them the pass. One of them said something into his headset and stared at us. He touched his hand to his earpiece then nodded at us as he handed Clay the pass. "Jameson, Spencer, take them through into the Processing Area."

I really didn't like the sound of that, but they had big guns, so I stayed quiet and followed the two guards through the huge gate. The Fifth Circle was as high as you could go, and very few people had ever been in it. It was reserved for the League, and I had never heard of anyone who had moved up into it. Once we got on the other side of the wall, we could see more guards stationed at intervals all around the wall, but you couldn't see them from the outside. A fat lot of good they were doing there. If the outer walls had as much firepower, life would be a lot more stable for a lot more people.

Inside the security building, another guard, this one with more stripes and medals than the other guys, instructed us to stand against the wall. They took their time searching us, and after a lot of groping and me holding my temper in check, the guy in charge declared us clean. He spoke into his radio and a few minutes later a tiny little man in a neatly pressed grey suit and round wire-rimmed glasses walked into the building. He smiled at me as he shook my hand. His hand was oddly cold, and it matched his eyes despite his smile. He spoke in an odd, clipped accent.

"Miss Wells, how nice to meet you at last. I'm David Evans, Mrs. Mayne's assistant. She's extremely excited to meet you."

I smiled and nodded as I shook his hand and pretended not to find it distasteful to touch him. "Thanks. It's nice to meet you too." I looked over at Clay, who was fidgeting and had tiny beads of sweat on his upper lip and brow. He held out his hand.

"Mr. Evans, I'm Clay Matthews. I'm Emily's—" He didn't get to finish as Evans cut him off.

"Agent, yes Mr. Matthews, I know who you are. Thank you for bringing Miss Wells so promptly. We'll take care of her from here. You may wait here."

Clay opened his mouth to protest but closed it at the finality of the look on Evans' face. Evans' head was inclined slightly, and he had a funny half smile as he waited for Clay to disagree. I shook my head at Clay, trying to convey that he didn't need to worry about me, but I knew he would. He obviously felt that without him there to do the talking I would make things worse. He was probably right.

I followed Evans out of the building. There was a little cart of some kind and another guard waiting for us. Evans climbed into the cart and smiled as he motioned for me to sit. "Please Miss Wells, sit. The ride won't take long."

I nodded as I sat in one of the seats. As soon as I did, the driver said something into his radio and took off. The little car was quiet except for a whirring noise as he drove it through another small gate. I don't know what I expected the Fifth Circle to look like, maybe for it to be made of gold with diamonds encrusted everywhere. It wasn't either of those things, but it was the most beautiful place I had ever seen. The houses were real houses, not cobbled together out of shipping containers or cabins, and they were clean and in perfect repair.

He stopped in front of a huge white house that was neat and clean. The lawn was lush and green. I had been outside the walls to scavenge so I had seen plenty of houses, but I had never seen one that nice. Everything I had ever seen was gray from weathering and overgrown with weeds and trees. I couldn't help but stare. I jumped in the air when water started squirting out of these weird little black stakes all over the lawn and was embarrassed when I heard Evans chuckle and pat me on the shoulder condescendingly. "Lovely, isn't it? It's so nice to see a bit of the Old World, don't you think? Cheers the soul."

I just stared at him. It didn't cheer the soul. It was out of place, and it was ridiculous considering the amount of people that could be fed and protected with the money it took to keep it in this condition. He opened the front door by waving a little white card at the door and when we stepped through, I felt cold. It was at least twenty degrees cooler inside, and I realized it was air-conditioned. I had never seen anything like it, but Danny and Charlie remembered a time when a cool building was common. Evans led me down the hallway and stopped in front of a heavy oak door. He smiled his cold smile again and asked me to wait as he went in first. He wasn't gone long before the door opened. He motioned for me to come in. The room was beautiful, all decorated in clean grey paint and elegant drapes on the windows. There was a huge oak desk in the middle of the room and the floor was covered in squishy white carpet. It was so bright and clean I didn't think I should step on it, and I hesitated to walk across the room. Evans was still smiling as he watched me look around. He stood by a door made all of windows and he opened it and motioned for me to go outside. "Mrs. Maynes is in the garden. This way please."

I stepped through the glass door onto some bricks and saw that there was a platform made from them. The backyard was as beautifully kept as the front, with flowers and big shade trees. Sitting at a small white table was the Commissioner. She was an older woman. How old, I couldn't guess because I was bad at that sort of thing, but she had jet-black hair that gleamed in the sunlight. Her face didn't look young, but didn't look wrinkled and old either. She was dressed in black pants and a light blue shirt that could have made her look relaxed except that it was perfectly ironed and stiff look-ing. She wore a pair of black half-glasses as she read a bunch of papers. I took in a big lungful of air and exhaled as I walked over to where she was sitting. Evans did the introduction. "Commissioner, Miss Wells," he said as he gave her a slight bow.

She looked over her glasses at him then smiled. Just like him, the smile didn't look genuine. She turned to me and gave me the same cold smile. "Thank you, David. You may leave us." Her voice had that same slight yet formal accent. She stood and shook my hand. "Miss Wells. Thank you so much for meeting with me today. Please, have a seat."

I shook her hand and noted the firm, cold handshake. "No problem," I said. "Nice place here."

She laughed as she poured a glass of tea and handed it to me. It had ice cubes in it. I had seen ice cubes twice in my life, including the other day when I soaked my ankle. "It is nice, thank you." She sat back down and sipped her drink. "You're probably wondering why I asked to see you."

I sniffed my tea and smelled nothing funny in it before I sipped it. "I think I have a pretty good idea why."

"Really?" she said. "Please tell me."

"It's about last Sunday's fight."

She nodded. "Yes. Yes, it is. I just wanted to make certain that you were all right. That was a nasty fall."

I knew she was full of shit, but I couldn't tell what the game was just yet. "Thanks for your concern ma'am, but really I'm fine. One of the hazards of the job."

"Well, not really. I suppose injury is quite common to you, but I've seen all your fights and I've never seen you sprain an ankle like that. Did the doctor look at it for you?"

I nodded and smiled. I'm sure my smile looked as fake

as hers did. "Yes ma'am. She gave me some medication. I'm fit and ready for Sunday."

"That's excellent to hear Emily. May I call you Emily?"

I kept my fake smile and nodded. "Sure. All my friends do."

"Yes, of course. Friends. And we are friends, Emily. I hope you know that. I would love for us to be good friends." She sat back in the chair and crossed her legs, then put her hands over her knee. Her hands were rough and not at all what I expected. They looked like my hands. "As your good friend, I have to tell you that I'm worried about you. You seem to take unnecessary risks."

I nodded at her. "I guess I can see how you think that."

"Your matches are no rules matches, difficult enough. Then you take on extra work? That's a great deal of risk for little reward, don't you think?" She tilted her head at me, still smiling that cold, creepy smile, as if she wanted to come across as a kindly mother, but the effect was more like a snake waiting to strike. "Now I realize that it was excellent theater, but Emily, you are too valuable and important to risk in that way. I must ask you, please for your own sake, think before you act in the future."

I nodded. "Yes ma'am. I just thought it was what the mob wanted. It's important to keep them happy."

She sipped her tea and nodded. "Quite right, but we must use discretion. What would we have done if you had been infected? Or permanently disabled? You're too important to lose."

"With all due respect ma'am, people pay to see me in the worst kind of danger. They're only there to see me lose."

She shook her head. "No, no, you've got that all wrong, Emily. They're paying to see you win. In you, they see themselves. Your triumph is their triumph."

She had that wrong, but what could I expect from somebody who lived in a place like this, so far from what the real world? She was as clueless as Claire.

"I'm not asking you to renegotiate your contract. Your matches are amazing. Truly wonders to behold. All I'm asking is for a little more caution." She smiled as she looked down at her papers. "If you're not worried about yourself," she looked at me and smiled again, "and you're young and invincible so I know you aren't worried for yourself, then please, think of your family. Think of Charles and little Sara. How would they feel about you taking these unnecessary risks?"

I felt cold and prickly as she said their names, as if my adrenaline had kicked in, just like a fight. Her eyes met mine, and she saw that I understood her perfectly. I felt like my blood was all pounding in my head and I tried to sip my tea without looking upset. "You're right ma'am. They wouldn't like it."

"Of course they wouldn't. So please, Emily, think

before you act next time. Many of us care about you. We don't want to see you get hurt." She finished her tea. "Now, is there anything that I can do for you? Better quarters? I can have more food delivered to you. Is there anything that you need? Anything at all?"

"No ma'am. I'm fine." I said as I finished my drink and set it on the table.

"If there is anything that you need, please let me know. I will make certain you get it."

I nodded at her and smiled. "I will, thank you."

She stood up and held out her hand again. I took it, and she placed her other hand on top of mine as she shook it. "I cannot wait to see your next match. I just know it's going to be spectacular. Please take care and I hope to see you again soon."

I returned the smile and nodded. "Thank you for the tea ma'am, and for your concern."

Evans led me back to Clay, who was sweating so much from nervousness that there were big stains under his arms. Neither one of us said anything until we got back through the gates and into the Third Circle. Before I went back into the dormitory, I hugged him and whispered, "You were right. I'm screwed."

7

Clay tried to get me a pass to go visit my family, but the request was denied. I thought briefly about sending a message to my new best friend, Commissioner Maynes, but if I did that, she would know exactly what I was trying to do and I doubted she would approve the request despite her claims to want to help me. Instead, I had to settle for the crappier option, which was to bring Charlie and Sara in for a regular visitation. I hated bringing them in for various reasons. It wasn't the safest place to talk. There were snitches everywhere, always listening and trying to use that information to their advantage. The other fighters were not to be trusted at all and I guess I couldn't blame them. They were using every skill they had to stay alive. If anyone overheard me talking to Charlie about what was going on, it would get back to the League immediately and I would sink deeper into the quicksand. I didn't have a choice, and The League knew that too because the visitor passes for Charlie and Sara were approved without any delay at all.

I was expecting to be ushered into the standard visit room. They didn't let anyone back to our rooms, and I wouldn't have wanted Sara back in the dorms with all the Cons anyway, so when I saw Clay coming down the hall with Charlie limping behind him and Sara skipping along, my heart started beating wildly as the adrenaline surged through my body. As soon as she saw me, Sara yelled and sprinted toward me. She left the ground from four feet away. I braced myself and winced as the pain shot through my ankle when I caught her.

"Easy Stretch. You trying to beat me up?"

She giggled and squirmed as I carried her inside my room. I threw her down on the bed and tickled her. "What are you doing here?" I looked up at Charlie and Clay and gave them a not so happy face.

"The Commissioner thought you might enjoy some more relaxed family time." Clay stood in the doorway. "So, enjoy."

"Yeah, it'll be real relaxed. We'll talk soon Clay," I scowled, and I waved at him as he started back down the hall. "How's the new place Charlie?"

He stared at me for a minute. That wasn't the conversation he thought we would be having. "It's good. Much nicer place."

"Good. You remember that place that Aunt Susan had? The one with the big oak trees?"

He looked at me again, puzzled. We didn't have an Aunt Susan, but to his credit, he caught on quickly. "Yeah. There was that tire swing. Lots of squirrels."

"What's a squirrel?" Sara asked.

"It's a rat with a furry tail," I said. "Yeah, there were tons of squirrels there. I wish we could go back there." I stared at Charlie pointedly.

"How would we ever get back there? That's pretty far." He looked over at Claire. "What is she doing here?"

"I live here," Claire said as she crossed her arms and stared back at him.

Charlie laughed. "Sure. What's going on Em?"

"She does stay here Charlie. Everyone else wants to kill her."

He laughed again. "And you are the only one who doesn't? That seems unlikely. You want to kill everyone."

I nodded. "Generally, yes, but not her. At least, not today. Look, we don't have a lot of time."

"To talk about Aunt Susan?"

"Yeah, and everything. We should make plans to go visit her."

"I just don't see how we do it."

"You let me worry about that. We'll do it someday." I tried to emphasize the two words. "Someday soon."

He nodded. "Ok, we will." He looked down at my ankle. "Are you hurt? It looked like you did a number on your leg in that match. That was idiotic, by the way. Why did you do that Emily?"

Sara piped up and pointed at Claire. "They didn't play fair! She should have gotten a blade. That's the rules. Em was helping."

I ruffled her hair. "Yeah, sort of. I'm fine Charlie. Don't worry about me. But I have to ask, what were you doing watching the fights?"

Charlie snorted. "You try keeping her from watching. It's impossible."

"Well don't watch Sunday. You're going to have other things to do," I said. "You get it?"

He shook his head and looked confused. Claire looked between us then nodded. "I'm sure you'll be busy. Don't you need to contact your aunt?"

Charlie stared at her for a while before answering. "Why are you even talking?"

"Because you're so slow." I said through clenched teeth. "Clay will help you contact her. Get it done Charlie. I'm serious."

"What's the rush? We haven't heard from Aunt Susan in a while."

I nodded. "Exactly. Something bad could happen to her. Something really bad could happen to her."

He still looked confused. "How are we going to make the trip?" He gestured toward Sara who was using the bunks like playground equipment, swinging like a monkey from top to bottom and back again. "Sara's never been outside the walls. My leg is junk. You're stuck in here."

"The best thing would be to go with a trade caravan. There has to be one going in the general direction of your Aunt's place," Claire said. Both Charlie and I looked at her as if she was speaking Chinese, but I had to admit that was a great idea.

"Yeah. The one going to Willow Creek would get you closest," I said. I snapped a finger at him and nodded to my bed. I stretched the blanket tight and in the fabric, I wrote:

GO OPPOSITE
I WILL FIND YOU

He nodded, as he finally understood the situation. "Yeah, it probably would. Won't be cheap Em."

"Clay will get you squared away." I grabbed Sara and started throwing her around as she screamed with laughter. "Go to him tomorrow. Don't wait Charlie. You miss that caravan and you'll have to wait awhile for the next one."

"I get that Emily. I'm not stupid, you know. I don't do idiotic things that endanger others." He looked between Claire and me.

"No, you don't do anything at all," I spat back. His face got red, and he was trying to find something to retort, but before he could keep the fight going, Claire stepped in.

"So, Sara, Em told me you got a new house and you're going to school. How do you like it?"

That shut both Charlie and I up as Sara told us all about their new place and her school classes and all the crap about the little kids in her neighborhood, all the normal stream-of-consciousness chatter of kids under ten. We wrestled around a bit and then it was time for them to go. Charlie shook his head as the guard came to escort them out.

"There's no point in telling you to be careful or anything else. You never listen."

"Not really, no." I hugged him and whispered in his ear. "I'm serious about this Charlie. You understand?"

He sighed and nodded. "Yes. I get it Emily."

I hugged Sara and held her tightly as she started to whimper and whine that she wanted to stay. "Look Stretch, you listen to everything Charlie tells you, got it?"

She had big tears in her eyes and I wiped them away. "Promise me."

She sniffed and wiped the tears from her eyes as she took the finger and shook it. "I promise but Em—"

I shook my head. "No buts Stretch. Good. I love you and I'll see you very soon," I said and waved as the guard took them down the hallway.

Claire came to stand next to me in the doorway. "I'm not sure he understands at all."

I shook my head. "No. He never does."

8

"I can't... I can't run anymore." Claire collapsed in a sweaty heap on the ground.

"Well, I guess you'll just die then," I said. I kicked a bit of the sand from the floor of the arena in her face and laughed when she sputtered and cursed me. "The zeds don't get tired. Not the Runners, and definitely not the shamblers, so if you think you can get tired, think again."

We had been training hard all week. The meeting with my new friend, Maynes, and with Charlie and Sara made me focus. My ankle was much better, possibly because I willed it to be, but also because Claire had been helping me with treatment and stretches. The swelling was gone, and the bruise had faded to a mix of light red and mustardy yellow. I could stand to run on it if Claire wrapped it up well, so we increased our sessions to twice a day. I wasn't 100%, but I was determined to be ready. If everything went according to plan, Charlie and Sara would be heading out with a trade caravan on Saturday. I had Clay arrange passage for them by booking two seats going north toward the Willow Creek settlement, then a cash deal with the shadier caravan going east to Oakmont. The guy who ran that was an old friend of Danny's from our scavenging days. He didn't keep the best records of passengers and trade cargo, mostly because he ran prostitutes and drugs with the occasional traveler who may or may not make it to the Oakmont station alive, but also I wasn't sure he could read. He wasn't exactly a bad person, but he wasn't a good citizen either, which meant that if he was given a nice wad of cash, he would take Charlie and Sara east and keep his pie hole shut about it.

The whole thing had been Claire's suggestion. I was stuck about the passage thing because I knew Charlie wouldn't have a chance just leaving on his own. His leg couldn't take it and he sucked at being out in the wild. Even when he had two good legs, he was terrible at fighting and bush craft. By the time I was five I was already more competent than he was at fifteen. I could set snares and start fires and could tell you a good defensive position from a bad one. Charlie still couldn't tell a bad campsite from a good one, let alone protect Sara from the zeds and everything else roaming around out beyond the walls, so he had to go with someone who could. I was ready to fight my way out of the dorms right then, but Claire had asked if I knew anyone who could take them and stay quiet about it until I could slip away.

She also helped me formulate a plan to get out of the arena after my match on Sunday so that Charlie and Sara would only have a day's head start on me. I could easily make up the distance and catch up with them in a couple of days. She had never included herself in these plans and that made me nervous. Was she planning on stringing me along then selling me out to save herself? That would make sense, and that's what 99% of the rest of the idiots in the dorm would do, but my gut told me that wasn't her angle. Part of me was telling myself that I was being a dumbass to trust her, but the other part of me wasn't even questioning her motives. That voice, for once, was louder than the skeptic, paranoid one.

Still there was a worry. It wasn't so much that Claire would rat me out, but more like I was being an ass by leaving her. We hadn't talked about her cure for zeds since that first night. I had made it clear that I thought she was full of shit and wouldn't listen to a bunch of crazy talk about it, but I was beginning to believe maybe she wasn't so crazy. She was incompetent at staying alive, sure, but I understood why, and that was made crystal clear after I actually saw the Fourth Circle. She knew her shit when it came to medicine, and somebody definitely wanted her dead, so I was thinking that maybe her zed cure wasn't a bunch of crazy talk after all. The thing was, it didn't change anything for me. My family was in danger and she wasn't my family. Not only that, but she would be useless in the wild—just another person for me to have to look out for—and I was going to have enough problems with my crippled brother and seven-year-old sister. I didn't need a pampered Fourth Circle who couldn't use weapons or run a hundred feet without being out of breath. At least that's what I kept telling myself as I tried to justify leaving her.

Claire stood up as she spit out dirt and tried to wipe her sweaty face. She shoved me, which didn't even move me, it actually made her unbalanced and she flopped back down into the dirt. "You're an ass, you know that?"

I nodded. "Of course. But I'm also alive. Get up and keep running."

She picked up a handful of dirt and threw it in my face. It was my turn to sputter. "You better fucking run now, because when I catch you, you're going to wish a zed got you."

I heard a bunch of laughter behind me. I turned as I finished wiping off my face and blinked a few times to clear my eyes. Rilla and her goons were enjoying the show. She sauntered over, accompanied by a new toady, one of the cons that came in when Claire did, named Ash.

"Aww, what's this? Lover's quarrel?" Rilla said.

"Looks like the honeymoon's over," Ash chimed in. She looked up at Rilla and punched her in the arm. "Hear what I said, Rilla? I said looks like the honeymoon's over, hehehehe."

"Yeah, she fucking heard you, dipshit. You just said it two seconds ago." I shook my head at Rilla. "Your dumb-asses get dumber by the day. You really know how to bring out the best in people Rilla."

Ash bristled up and came to stand in between Rilla and me. "Did you just call me a dipshit?"

The girl wasn't exactly little, about 5'7", and she was decently thick, but she was still shorter than me and I outweighed her by at least fifteen pounds so I wasn't intimidated by her bowed-up back.

"Yeah, I did call you a dipshit, you dipshit. Do I need to say things twice to you like you just did? Is that some kind of language requirement for you?"

There was a crowd starting to gather now and Claire had stood up and dusted herself off. She put a hand on my arm. "Em... come on."

"Yeah. Better listen to your girlfriend," Ash said. "You should save it for Sunday. You're gonna need it from what I heard." Ash looked down at my ankle then at Rilla and grinned. "Hehheh. You hear that boss? I said she's gonna need all she got because her—"

Before she could finish her double speak, I grabbed

her hair and slammed her nose with my fist. It exploded like an over-ripe tomato and she gurgled as the blood gushed out. I kept hold of her hair and looked at Rilla. "What do you think she was trying to say?" Rilla didn't answer; she just stood there and stared.

Ash spit a bunch of blood out and coughed. "Ahm a fuhckin kill you."

"What was that?" I put my ear next to her and looked at Rilla. "Did you hear that? Maybe I should help her clear her throat." I drug Ash over to the wooden weapons rack, whacked her face into the side of it twice, then let her fall to the ground. She was moaning and mumbling curses at me. "I think maybe she has some concerns about my health." I bent down and acted as if I was listening to her. "Yeah, that's it. She thinks I'm hurt." I kicked her solidly in the ribs with my bad foot. "If I was hurt, could I do that?" I kicked her again. "I doubt it. Couldn't stand to do that at all." I kicked her one last time and felt her ribs crack. She was a bloody, heaving mess. I walked back over to Rilla and ignored the pain in my ankle and fist. "Did you hear what I said, *boss*? I said, I doubt it. Couldn't stand to do that at all." I stood there for a few seconds, looking Rilla directly in the eye.

She blinked first.

"Leave her dumb ass. The guards can deal with her," Rilla said. She waved off two of her other dipshits who were trying to pick up what was left of Ash. She looked back at me and at Claire, then she smiled. "Good luck on Sunday," she said, then she walked away, taking her group with her.

Claire knelt beside Ash and checked her out. "Jesus, you almost killed her!"

I shrugged. "Yeah. So?"

"So? You can't just go around beating people!"

"Who says? Them?" I looked over at the guards. They were laughing, highly amused by the whole thing. "You think they care if some criminal junkie dipshit gets the shit kicked out of them in here?"

"There was no reason for you do this!" Claire stood up and balled her fists. She had little points of red on her cheeks and her jaw was clenched.

"Look, I guess you people in the Fourth Circle just sit around having tea and cookies all day, but down here in the real world, we have to beat people up sometimes. Sometimes these people deserve it. This one did. She was an asshole. She started some shit that she couldn't finish." I motioned to the guards to come and take Ash to the infirmary. "When you do that, this is what happens."

"She was being a mouthy jerk. She didn't deserve to have her face bashed in because of it."

"She deserved exactly that. She called me out, and she found out what happens when you do that."

"Oh is that right? Somebody says something you don't

like and you think an appropriate response is to beat them to death?"

I nodded. "If the something said implies that I'm weak. Yes. I couldn't let her get away with that. Not here and not now. And what's with this concern all of a sudden? You weren't full of all this human kindness when I beat up Rilla for you."

"I didn't ask you to do that!"

"No, you didn't, but if I hadn't, guess what you'd be doing right now? If you were still alive, that is, and not a resident of the zed pens." She looked at me but didn't answer, just opened her mouth a few times as her face got red with embarrassment. I laughed a mirthless laugh. "Yeah. Way worse than that, sweetheart. And think what they would have done to you if I had backed down and they thought for a second that they could take me? You think you'd be safe? Think again."

The guards dragged Ash out and we headed back inside. "I-I... no, but Emily, this just isn't any way to live," Claire said. She closed her eyes and shook her head.

"It's not living. It's surviving. They're not even close to the same thing." I motioned toward the outside. "But that's what it takes to survive in here and out there. You can't show weakness. You can't turn the other cheek. The first time you do, somebody is going to stick a knife in it."

"I don't think I can be like that."

I shrugged. "Then I guess you're going to die."

"I guess so. Maybe you'd be better off."

"Maybe? Not maybe. Definitely. But the problem is, *I* can't be like *that*." I flopped down on my bed, put my ankle up, and winced.

Claire sighed and started to unwrap it. "I don't think your survival instinct is as strong as you think it is." She looked at the foot and poked it a little. "I'm going to see if that guard Vance will get you some ice."

"No. No way. Nobody can see that. Just give me some of those pills."

She shook a couple of the pills out and gave them to me. "Stay off it for the rest of the day."

I sank back into the pillows and heard her bedsprings squeak as she got into her rack. "No worries there."

"You're going to have to leave me here, you do realize."

I let out a long breath then turned to face the wall.

I didn't answer her.

9

We passed the week exchanging the bare minimum of words necessary. We couldn't really talk about my escape plan because I didn't want even a hint of it to be overheard, and if we didn't talk about that, then we really didn't have much else to say. I kept thinking that I should say something about leaving her, but I didn't know what I should say. She understood what was going to happen and nothing I said was going to make the outcome different, so I just didn't say anything. The truth was that without me, Claire was totally vulnerable. If she made it through her fight, she would still have to deal with Rilla and her group, which was going to be much more difficult than dealing with an arena full of zeds. She wouldn't last the night and that was my fault. I tried not to think about that too hard.

I had a routine every Sunday morning before a fight. I got up, ran a bunch of laps, and warmed up. It was especially important to do it because nobody could know that it was different from any other Sunday. I kept to my routine; I ran and got warmed up just as I always did, then we were ushered into the waiting room. It was more like a holding pen I suppose—everyone just stayed in it as the matches went down. One by one, everyone had their fight until Claire and I were the only ones left in the room. We listened to the mob screaming as the other fights went on and the sounds of fighters screaming if the zeds overtook them. I blocked it out, but Claire was upset by it.

"How can you just sit there and listen?" she asked as she paced the room.

"I don't."

She exhaled a huge breath and looked like she was going to cry. "I'll never get used to this. Never."

"I don't know what to say to you," I said.

She paused and stared at me for what seemed like an eternity. "Whatever happens to me is not your fault. You do what you have to do. I am not your responsibility."

"I know that."

"No you don't. You took responsibility for me that first day and you haven't let go since. You have to let go."

I walked over and stood in front of her. "You'll make it through your fight. When you get back to the dorms, shank somebody at dinner. Anybody. They think you won't kill anyone so they aren't afraid of you. Make them afraid."

She laughed and shook her head. "I won't do that, and you know it."

"I think you will. You want to live and you're not stupid," I said.

"It's your way. It's not my way."

I grabbed her face and held it firm. "It's not my way. It's their way. You either can play or be played." I let go of her face and took a step back and looked down at my feet. "Thank you for helping me with everything. I mean with my ankle."

She nodded. "Thank you for saving my life. Lots of times."

"That sounded like genuine gratitude. Are you sick?"

"Probably."

We both laughed a little then turned to look as the door swung open. Clay and two handlers entered. He looked grim.

"What are you doing here?" I asked.

Before he answered, the handlers pulled out a long chain between two leather belts. They didn't say anything as they fastened one around Claire and locked it with a little lock. They moved toward me and I bristled.

"Come near me with that and it will be your last act," I said to the bigger one. "Clay, what the hell is going on?"

"It's a chain match. You go in together." He looked down at the ground.

"Bullshit. I'm not doing this."

Clay didn't look up. "You agreed to no rules. The League insisted."

"And you didn't try to stop them?" Claire asked him.

"How would I do that? This is their game." Clay finally looked at me. "I'm sorry kid, but if anybody can make this work, you can."

There was no use protesting. If they had to call in ten more people, they would put the belt on me and they wouldn't be gentle about it. I nodded. "Hurry up." I held my hands in the air as they fastened the belt and locked it. Claire and I were connected by about ten feet of chain. "Clay, the other thing?"

He nodded. "Everything is ok. Just make it through this one and the payday will be

huge."

"Oh, I will. You can bet on that."

He smiled at me. The first genuine smile I had ever seen from him. "I always bet on you, kid," he said as he and the handlers left.

I gathered up the chain. It wasn't the heaviest grade, but it wasn't light either. I couldn't break it, at least not yet. Claire was tugging it and she looked panicked.

"What-what are we going to do?" she asked, her voice shaky and small.

I shrugged. "Whatever we have to do. The plan hasn't changed. I'm getting out of here."

"How? You can't do this with me chained to you."

"It will be difficult, but not impossible. Do what I say, no questions."

She nodded. "Emily..."

"What?"

"I'm scared."

"Don't be," I said as the big wooden gate opened, flooding the room with the light and sound of the arena. "They're the ones who should be scared." I grabbed her hand, and we walked into the light.

The mob went insane when we entered. They were stomping and screaming so loud that the arena shook. I plastered a big cocky grin on my face as I walked out into the middle of the ring. I waved and saluted them, turning so that I faced each side of the crowd once. I held up the chain and Claire's hand and the mob went nuts again. The announcer was doing his thing, trying to hype the game, but they were practically frothing at the mouth, and had little need of him to hype them more. Finally, the directive came to open the chest, and I made the same show of doing it as I always did. I paused, slowly opened it, and when I did, I got the first real feeling of panic that I had since that day in the Commissioner's place. Inside the chest was a single sheet of paper. I picked it up and read it. It said:

When life hands you lemons...
Best of Luck,
C. Maynes

I looked up in the League box and there was the Commissioner. She smiled down at us and gave a little salute. I tried to control my anger and fear as I folded the paper neatly and tucked it into my pocket. I planned to make her eat that letter later. I looked up again and returned her smile. I saluted her back. The mob went nuts, pounding on whatever structure was available—the floor, the chain link, the Plexiglas. Even the other fighters, the ones that had survived their matches, were pounding on the wooden rails of the box and screaming.

"Emily, what are we going to do?" Claire was right in my ear.

"Well, I'm not entirely sure," I said. I slammed the chest closed and smiled. "Hopefully not die." I touched the chain. "We'll use this. Just don't panic."

She swallowed hard and nodded.

We both looked toward the zed pen and heard the clang as the metal gate swung open. One runner came bursting out followed by a herd of twenty shamblers. I grinned. I knew what we were going to do.

"Focus on the runner. Take him out first," I yelled. I took a few steps away from her and shook the chain. "Follow?"

She nodded.

He was a fresh runner, just a few hours into the infection, and he was mad. He sprinted toward us screaming and growling. The mob was breathless. When he got to us, he stopped and looked confused. He didn't know which one of us to eat first. He started toward Claire, but I put my hands up and shouted. "Hey! Nope, right here buddy!" I waved my arms and taunted him, and he stopped moving toward her and launched himself toward me. I caught him, and we landed on the ground with him on top of me. I got my knees between us and was able to keep him from biting me, but I wouldn't be able to hold him for long. "Loop the chain around his neck," I yelled to Claire.

She could barely lift it, but she did it, then she yanked him off me. He scrambled around and tried to get the chain off his neck as he screamed and spit. I was up quickly and got on one side of him. Claire was on the other. She looked at me with horror as she realized what I intended to do. "Emily... no."

I smiled and nodded. "Yes. On the count of three, pull as hard as you can. One-Two-Three!"

When we pulled in opposite directions, his head didn't quite pop off his body as if I thought it would, but it almost did. The chain cut deep into his neck and killed him quickly as it broke his neck. The mob screamed in appreciation.

I un-looped it from him. He would reanimate and that would be perfect. I grabbed his arms. "Claire, come on, drag him over here."

She winced as she handled the gore-coated chain. She kept it from impeding me as I dragged him to the place just beneath the opened fighter's box. The herd of shamblers had finally gotten down to where we were and were moaning and grabbing for us. I kicked the first few out of the way then looped the chain around the waist of one. He was a crispy one. When we pulled the chain, he split neatly in half and made a weird dry crunchy sound, like a cornhusk. He was still moaning, but just kind of rolling around. I nodded to the next one. "Keep doing it."

Claire grasped the chain and nodded. She kept a grim look of determination on her face as we cut all the shamblers in half. Some were dry old guys—like the first one— and some were still kind of gushy and juicy, which was messy, but eventually we got them all halved. The mob was laughing at this point because I suppose it was funny watching the zeds come apart like they did, either crispy and crackly or soft with lots of ooze that spurted out on us every once in a while. By the end of it, we were both black with decaying blood and there were twenty half zeds crawling around. The match wasn't over until we killed them all. At least that's what the rules said, but I had agreed to a no rules match. If they could make up their own, so could I.

I grabbed one of the dry ones arms and tested his weight. He was light. I grinned at Claire.

She looked at me then at the stands of people. "You wouldn't."

My answer was to toss the half a zed up over the chain link and into the crowd. I did it twice more before they realized what was happening and started to panic. The half-zeds could still bite and they were grabbing ankles and causing the distraction I needed. I hurled a juicy one up into the fighter's box and sent them all scrambling, which cleared out the immediate area. All over the arena, the mob was screaming and panicking. Streams of people fought with each other to get out of the stands, too worried now about flying zeds to think about anything but escape.

I tossed one final one up into the box and looked at Claire. "Let's go." I grabbed her and boosted her up the wall. She had a hard time, but she finally got up and over. She was standing there looking down at me. "Pull the chain as tight as you can." She nodded then disappeared, and I felt the chain tighten, pulling me against the wall. I jumped, grabbed it, and stilled my feet then I pulled myself up the chain until I could grab the top of the wooden wall. I scrambled around awkwardly until I got one leg up and over then pulled myself into the box. I landed on top of Claire. We straightened ourselves out and gathered the chain.

"How are we going to get out of here?" she asked. The crowd screamed, and the stands shook as the people tried to get out.

"As fast as we can," I said as I looped as much of the chain as I could around myself. "Head for that exit." She followed awkwardly, the chain between us made it difficult to move quickly and we were constantly bumping into each other. We passed into the crowd and I shoved people out of the way as we moved toward the stairs that led down to the ground level.

"Wait, Em. This isn't going to work. We have to get these belts off."

I stopped and stared at her. "Yeah, no shit, but how do you plan on doing that right at this moment?"

"I don't know. Can we cut it?"

"With what? I don't have a knife."

I looked up and saw a handler running down the hall toward us. I grinned. He would have something useful. He smiled when he saw us and pulled out his baton. "You girls are in a bunch of trouble."

"That is a fact," I said. Before he could do anything, I brained him with the chain. He fell to the ground and shook. I grabbed his baton and keys and found a pocketknife in his pants. It wasn't going to cut through the leather quickly. We would need to buy some time. I turned and headed back down to the fighter's box.

"What are you doing? That's back inside!" Claire screamed at me.

I nodded. "Yeah. For now." I dangled his keys and held up the knife. "We need a place to cut these belts off."

"This is a stupid idea."

"Yeah, well you don't seem to be coming up with anything better, so shut up." I dragged her back into the box then we climbed down into the ready room. We could still hear the thundering of the panicked crowd, but there was nobody in the room. I pulled out the pocketknife and grabbed my belt. It seemed like it took forever to saw through the leather but in reality it was just a few minutes. Once I got the belt off I started toward Claire, but she held up a hand. "Stop. You should go now."

"Don't be an idiot," I said as I grabbed her belt.

"I can't help you. I'll only slow you down. The smart play is to leave me." She grabbed my hand and stopped the knife.

I knew she was right. Even if we got the belts off, she would still be chained to me. She would still make it harder. The smart thing to do would be to leave her there. I looked at her for a moment. Then I smiled.

"Probably so, but I used up all my smarts getting to this point, so I guess you're coming with me." I resumed cutting off her belt amid her sputtering protests. "You can't stay here Claire, not after all this. At least with me you have a chance. Besides, you know stuff. You aren't totally useless like I originally thought you were."

"Thanks for that ringing endorsement."

I finished with her belt and tossed her the keys as I grabbed the handler's baton. "You're in charge of locks. I'll take care of any problems."

She sighed wearily as she unlocked the door. "This is a terrible idea."

I smiled as I smacked the baton against my hand. "No way. Now they're the ones who are in big trouble." I headed out the door and to the right, the way that led out.

10

The first handler we encountered went down when I whacked him in the head with the baton. He hit the ground with a very satisfying thud.

"Did you kill him?" Claire yelled. She knelt to examine him. I joined her, but I was going through his pockets. I found another set of keys, a lighter, and a pair of handcuffs. I pocketed them all.

"No, I didn't." I also grabbed his baton. "But so what if I did?" I kicked him. There were decent handlers and shitty handlers. The decent ones treated us like people. With the shitty ones, the best you could hope for was indifference and slight contempt. The worst case was they treated you like property to do with what they liked. This guy was one of the shitty ones. He had arrangements with some of Rilla's crew, and if they didn't want to deal, he took what he wanted. While he had never messed with me, I had seen him go after some of the new girls who weren't tough enough to keep him away or smart enough to deal. He deserved a lot worse than I had given him. "This guy is an asshole."

Claire stood up and rolled her eyes at me. "You can't just go around beating up people you think are assholes."

"Actually, I can. But let's discuss your ethical objections to my escape plan after we've avoided getting captured." I started down the hallway toward the handler's exit—a door led out into a holding area where they brought you when you were locked up. We had keys to get out, but the trick was going to be making it through the room if there was a squad inside.

"There has to be a better way." Claire shook her head and crossed her arms.

I grabbed her and shoved her up against the wall. "I have to get out of here. If I don't find Charlie and Sara, they will both die. If that means some of these assholes die, so be it. I take care of me and mine. That's how this world works, so shut the fuck up and do what I tell you."

"You should just leave me here."

"No way. They won't make it quick or painless. And besides, you know the plan. They will get it out of you. I'll be done. You're coming if I have to knock you out and carry you."

She huffed out a resigned breath and nodded. "This discussion isn't over. Do you actually have a plan or are you just going to beat up everyone we see?"

"Even I won't be able to take out a room full of handlers. We need to figure out something else."

She thought for a moment. "Hostage?"

I shook my head. "I don't think these jerks care enough about each other for that to work. We have keys to get out. We need a distraction."

"Can you get into the infected holding area from here?" she asked.

"Yes. It's at the other end of the arena though."

"Let's go. I'll explain when we get there," she said.

We headed down the hallway in the opposite direction. The zed pen was all the way around on the opposite end from where we were, next to the fighter green room and the dorm entrance. We didn't encounter any handlers going that direction, but when we got to the door to the pen, there were two guards stationed. The first one didn't have time to get his baton free because I used mine to whack him in the nose. I clubbed him over the head as he bent over and he was out.

The second one was huge—at least 6'5"—and weighed easily 300 pounds. Instead of a club, he had a long, wicked-looking bayonet. It was twelve inches, and the edge gleamed. I grinned at him and motioned him forward. If he got me with it, at least I was in the right place, near the zed pen. He took a couple of swings and I ducked. He might have been big, but he wasn't a knife fighter. He was just a big idiot with a big knife. "This is gonna to be fun," he said. "They'll give me anything I want for bringing you in." He nodded toward Claire as he circled. "Bet they let me keep her."

"Hey, you got my knife," I said as I mirrored him.

"Oh, don't worry, I'm gonna give it to you, sweetheart."

The knife crashed into the wall where I had been a microsecond before. He was slow though, and by the time he swung again, I had moved around him. He missed and overbalanced. I ducked, skirted behind him, and hit him in the kidney with both my batons. He screamed and fell to his knees and when he did, I hit him in the throat. He immediately fell over, clutching at his windpipe as he wheezed and choked. I casually picked up the knife and twirled it in my hand as I smiled. He looked up at me in terror and panic as he gasped and tried to breathe.

"You are a man of your word." I winked at him then I hit him in the face with my baton. He gave a gurgle then went quiet. I took a belt off the smaller handler and put it on. The batons tucked in nicely. Claire was looking at the big guy grimly. "See?" I said.

She nodded. "You may be correct, but that doesn't mean I have to like this."

"You'll get used to it. Now what is your plan?"

"How are the infected housed? The sick are mixed in here with the reanimated?"

I shook my head. "No way. The runners are in one. Shamblers in another." I pointed to the two doors. "You can't keep them together. They'll go after each other."

"So we can't mix them and we can't fool the infected, but we can fool the reanimated." She motioned toward our clothes that were still covered in muck from the arena.

I understood what she wanted to do, but we weren't covered in nearly enough dead blood and guts to fool the shamblers. Moreover, that wouldn't fool the runners at all. They tore into anything that moved, living or dead. "Okay, well we don't stink enough to fool them."

She nodded. "Oh, I know. We need more blood." She motioned toward the door. "We can't use the guard. He hasn't been rotten, but we can get another corpse."

"You want to wrangle a shambler, cover ourselves in rotten goo, then what, let loose the whole herd of them?" I looked at her in awe. I have to say, I was impressed with the plan.

"Yes. We will lead them down the hallway to the intake room and set them loose. We'll slip out in the confusion." She looked between the two doors. "Now which is which?"

"I have no idea. You can't tell from the arena. They all

come out of one gate." I looked at the two doors for some clue, but there weren't any signs to help me decide which door to open. "I guess we'll just have to open one and see."

"You have the knife. I'll open the door." She picked the door on the right and stood by it. "Give me the keys."

I handed her the keys and stood right by the door. "Unlock it, then we're going to pull it open and, check. Be ready to close it in a hurry if they're runners."

When she opened the door, the freaking runner must have been right by it, listening to the racket we made, because as soon as it opened, the runner flung herself out the crack and knocked Claire back. Then the thing rammed into me and sent me flying, both of us in a tangle of limbs as she snarled and snapped at me. Her mouth got so close to my neck that I swear I felt her lips graze me, and I could smell her rotten stinking breath as she spit gobs of froth and black shit all over me. The knife went flying, but by some miracle of physics, I managed to get my arms up and keep her just far enough away to prevent a bite. She was strong and persistent as she lunged and gnashed at the air. She had me pinned down, and I couldn't get my legs up between us. I felt my arms shaking as I struggled to hold her away and figure out some way out from under her at the same time. I knew I didn't have long. That's when the bayonet came poking out of her eye and she went slack. Claire panted as she struggled to pull the knife free from the thing's skull. I scrambled out from under it as it twitched a final time.

Claire had managed not only to stab it but also close the door so no other runners got out. I was breathing hard, and the adrenaline was coursing through me as I shook out my arms and tried to calm myself. "Well, I guess that was the wrong door."

Claire gave a little laugh. "I suppose so. So left one was the better choice."

"Remind me never to let you gamble. You suck at it." I shoved her out of the way as I put my foot on the zed's head and pulled the knife free. Claire had shoved it in all the way to the hilt. I never would have thought it possible. I wiped the blade clean on the runner's shirt and nodded toward the other door. I'm going to get one out. Close the door quick."

This time, the shambler was right by the door, but slow, so I just grabbed it by its shirt and yanked it through the door. It moaned and snapped, but compared to the runner it was in slow motion and almost funny. Claire shoved the door closed, and I put the thing out of its misery. Thankfully, it was a juicy one, not desiccated and dry so we had plenty of goo to work with after I cut her open. I gagged as we smeared the putrid shit all over us. Claire threw up twice, but she still managed to cover herself well enough to fool a whole herd.

"What if this infects us?" I asked.

Claire shook her head. "It doesn't really transmit like that. It has to be a bite."

"So why do they bleach us down?"

She shrugged. "I mean, it's a good precaution, but I never found evidence that it transmitted like this. Think about it. How many times have you been sprayed? There's no way you've kept it out of your eyes and mucous membranes. If you could get infected from this, you would have been infected a long time ago."

"So they're lying to us about how this works?"

"Yes. They're lying to you about a great many things." She finished smearing some black fluid on her neck and stood up. "Avoid your face if you feel weird about it."

I cleaned off the knife and nodded. "Ok, let's get on with this." She opened the shamblers' door and backed away from it. They immediately perked up and sniffed the air, but looked confused. They could still smell lingering human, but the stench of decay was so strong in the room that they didn't quite know what to do.

"What the hell do I do?" I said through clenched teeth. "How are they going to follow us?"

Claire picked up the fallen handler's baton and banged the metal desk a few times. Then she let out a terrible moan that really got their attention. They moaned back in answer and when she did it again, the whole bunch of them, probably twenty, moaned again in unison and began to stream out of the doorway.

"Start moving down the hall. Slowly," Claire said in a calm, soft voice. "Move like them."

I nodded and shuffled down the hall. Claire moaned a few more times, and they followed us down the hall just like a herd of cattle. My heart was racing, and I struggled to keep the slow, even pace that mimicked the way they moved. My instinct was to run. It seemed like it took forever to get them all the way down the hall, but they picked up a little steam when they started to smell the fresh human scent coming from the dorms. When we got to the door to the intake room, they all stopped and moaned as they sniffed the air. Claire handed me the keys, and I fumbled around as I tried to find the one that opened the door. One of the shamblers, an old woman with white glazed eyes and half her cheek missing, stopped beside me. She sniffed me and gave a confused moan that agitated the rest of them and they moaned back.

"Emily, please hurry up," Claire said in her quiet, calm voice. "The smell is wearing off us."

"No shit," I answered back in the same tone of voice. "I'm trying but there are thirty keys here."

The old lady sniffed me again and moaned, but I had finally found the right key. I slowly put it in the lock and opened the door.

The whole herd moaned excitedly as they flowed through the door. The screaming, cursing, and sounds of chairs and other stuff hitting the floor as all the handlers in the room panicked told us that the trick worked. We followed the excited zeds into the room and pushed our way through the crowd. I ignored all the screams and pleas for help as I used the key to unlock the final door. I slammed it shut behind us and we found ourselves out in the Second Circle.

11

I breathed a sigh of relief as my back made solid contact with the door. We made it out. The handlers had all they could deal with inside as the mob of shamblers that we let loose kept them occupied. I could just barely hear the screams and groans through the heavy metal door. I wasn't the least bit upset by it and Claire didn't seem to be either. I had to find Charlie and Sara. Nothing else mattered.

Claire was busy scanning the crowd that was rushing around outside still panicked by the thought of the zeds that we tossed into the stands. Logically, those zeds really couldn't do much damage, being cut in half, but crowds of people tend to not think logically when you fling moaning, snapping corpses into their midst. Their instinct—which had kept them alive so far—was to run, and run they did.

Throngs of people streamed from the various exits of the arena. Some of them were from the First and Second Circles, dressed in worn and dirty clothes, and some Upper Circle people, Third and maybe Fourth Circlers, in cleaner and in newer duds. They exited out of any place they could and some of them had come out inside the Second Circle instead of where they had entered. They looked appalled to be in there. Mothers were hugging their children tight to them, almost as afraid of the denizens of the Second Circle as they were of the zeds.

I tried to clear my mind of the chaos so that I could figure out how to get out of there. We still had to go through the Second and First circles before we got out into the wild where we could track the caravan. We had several problems. First, we would have to get through a security check just to get out—one from Second to First—which would be pretty major. Getting out of the last wouldn't be as big a deal. Nobody really cared if you got in or out of the First Circle. They were more concerned with you having the cash to get into the second. Guards would have to be dealt with and even I knew that I couldn't just leave a path of dead security in my wake. The second problem we had was that we had no supplies. I had some decent weapons—

the big knife and the batons—which would be ok, but we had no supplies. I didn't need much, but a few things would be helpful, like a canteen and some cordage. Third, we had no transport. The caravan we needed to find was slow; it was horse-drawn, and they were the big slow draft horses, but it was still faster than we could walk and it had a full day's head start. We had no shot at getting anything motorized. Gasoline was scarce. The League hoarded it and kept the vehicles under heavy security. Fourth, we were conspicuous. Not only were we covered in zed blood and entrails but also I was one of the most famous people in the city. Big posters of me were plastered all over the outside of the arena, and I was a household name. I wouldn't get ten feet away before somebody recognized me.

Claire had obviously come to the same conclusion because she shook her head as she looked at me. "The first thing we have to do is get you covered up."

I nodded in agreement. "Yeah, and get cleaned up. They'll brain us because they'll think we're zeds." I looked around and saw an alley. "In there for now."

We kept close to the side of the arena and worked our way to the alley. It was a camp, but the only people there were a couple of old timers, too old to be easily moved. Everyone else had fled or hadn't made it back to the camp yet. Claire wrinkled her nose at the strong smell of sweat and human waste, but to me it didn't seem that bad. I had spent my time in the First Circle, so this place seemed like a palace to me. They had a decent cooking area and little alcoves for sleeping that had solid corrugated metal walls and roofs. There was a barrel of grey water that they probably recycled for washing. I grabbed a rag from one of the sleeping pallets and immediately began to scrub the blood off my face. Claire gagged as she looked at the water, but it was still not as disgusting as we were so she didn't say anything as she grabbed a piece of cloth and did the same. I scrounged around and found a couple of shirts for us. They were dirty but less filthy than the ones we were currently wearing. I stripped off my gore-covered shirt, threw it into one of the piles of refuse, and changed into the new one. Claire's was about three sizes too big and hung to her knees. She sniffed it and rolled her eyes but didn't complain as she gathered the ends and knotted it so she could walk.

"We have to cover your face," she said after she had finished.

"Yeah. Agreed," I said. I looked around the camp. I hated the idea of taking from these people. They didn't have much, and I knew what they had to do just to get the few things they had, but I really didn't have many options.

"Just take what you need."

Both Claire and I jumped when the old woman spoke. She sat with her back against the wall, a tiny little lump under some filthy blankets. She looked ancient. Her shriveled old hands were spotted with more than just dirt, and they shook as she clutched her rags.

"Ma'am. I'm not a thief but—" I held up a threadbare blanket.

She stopped me with a raised old claw of a hand. "I know who you are. Saw you fight once. Just take it."

"Thank you," I said. I whipped out the knife, cut the blanket into a couple of wide strips, then did the same with another one that I found. I tossed them to Claire and began to wrap my head up with the other. I knelt beside the old woman and shook her hand. "Take care ma'am."

"You watch yourself." Her eyes were surprisingly clear for one so old. "Best go now. Camp will be back once everyone calms."

I nodded and turned to Claire who had just draped the cloth over her head. "Isn't there anything else here we can use?" she asked.

"We don't have time to look." I flattened against the wall as a group of Handlers ran by the opening of the alley. They were covered in blood and they were yelling at each other to hurry up and get to the gate. "Great. They're headed to the gate. Any bright ideas of how to get past them?"

"Maybe," she said.

I didn't like the maybe, but her ideas had been every bit as good as mine, so I didn't say anything as I led her to the gate between the Second and First Circles. There were throngs of people trying to get in and out. The Handlers that we saw go by the alley were forming a checkpoint that augmented the one that was normally there. Usually it was no big deal to go from a higher circle to a lower one—in fact, they usually didn't even stop you—but today they were checking everyone. No way was I getting out if we stood in that line. The gate was a livestock gate, about fifteen feet wide, but they closed it so that only two people could go through at a time. The people from the arena were already freaking out because of the delay in getting to safety—if you could call the First Circle safety. People were shouting at the Handlers and pushing toward the exit. The Handlers were cracking skulls if anybody acted up, and they were searching every single person, no exceptions.

"Yeah, this is going to be a problem," I said quietly. "No way are we getting past them."

Claire sighed heavily and nodded. "No, not unless we can distract them." She looked around. "Do you think a fire would do it?"

"Not likely. These guys don't care if it burns to the ground." I watched the crowd grow less patient and a little shoving start. I smiled. "I think I have an idea. Stay close to me and be ready to go."

"What are you going to do?"

"Give things a little push," I said. "Just be ready to

run." Her mouth formed words as if she wanted more explanation, but she thought better of it and just nodded.

Standing a few people ahead of me was a meaty looking guy who was complaining loudly about how long it was taking to move. I maneuvered myself behind him, took a deep breath, then shoved him as hard as I could. He lost his balance and crashed into the group ahead, who started yelling and shoving him back. He didn't even turn around to look at me because he was busy pushing and yelling back at the group in front.

It didn't take long for things to escalate. The whole crowd, already on edge from the arena, snapped. Fights and shoving matches broke out all over. The angry mob pulsated, surged, and became an unstoppable wave of bodies. I grabbed Claire's hand and kept us moving toward the gate as the people around us yelled and punched at each other. The Handlers couldn't do anything but get back out of the way as the tide of people exploded through the gate and into the First Circle.

Once we got through the gate, people dispersed. They were still fighting, but we weren't so tightly packed. I was able to duck around the individual skirmishes and avoid being punched. Claire wasn't so lucky. A rough looking woman flew into her, knocking them both to the ground. She must have blamed Claire or was just spoiling for a fight because she rolled on top of Claire and pummeled her. All Claire could do was get her hands up to protect her face as the woman cursed and punched her for all she was worth. I grabbed the woman by the scruff of her neck and hauled her off Claire, then threw her back into the sea of fists. I held out a hand to Claire who cursed too as she hopped up. Her nose was bloody, but she mopped at it with her scarf and we got the hell out of there. I didn't know if the Handlers would follow us out into the slums of the First Circle, but I wasn't about to chance it.

Claire stopped and looked around. I guess if I had never seen the squalor of the First Circle, I would have stopped too. The place was a filthy maze of tarps and waste. The little tin alcoves in the alley were palaces compared to the cardboard shacks and tents that littered the First Circle. They weren't laid out in any discernable pattern, just scattered around amidst a sea of trash and filth. I grabbed her hand and pulled her along toward the outer fence.

"This is… people live here?" she asked.

"They try to," I said. Claire screamed and jumped as she stepped on a rat that squealed and scurried into a pile of trash. There were lots of them around, but they had to be quick. If they were caught, they ended up in a stew. "It's just a rat. Keep moving. There are way worse things than them out here."

"Like what?"

I pulled out my knife and scanned the little section. There were dirty people eyeing us suspiciously and whispering as we moved. "Like people who want to jump us and take our stuff. Like your buddy Rilla." There was a group of three people huddled around a sparse looking campfire as we passed. They were thin and reedy looking, filthy, with crusty black hands and greasy, smeared faces.

"We don't have anything worth taking," Claire said quietly.

"Yeah, well they don't know that. They might miss something." The group followed, talking loudly behind us.

"Couple of babies out for a stroll," one of the men cackled with laughter. "What did these pretties bring us?"

I ignored them and kept moving. I was hoping they would drop off once we got closer to the gate, but they didn't. They kept a measured pace behind us, catcalling and speculating about us loudly. When we reached the fence and final gate, I saw another group of three clustered around it. They called out and whistled to the group behind us.

"Great. A gang," I said as I stopped.

"Gate toll for these babies," the mouthy guy said. He grinned, showing a mouth of rotten black teeth.

"I don't think you're in charge here," Claire said huffily. "Let us by immediately."

The whole bunch started cracking up and making fun of her. Actually, I would have done the same. She sounded ridiculous, and she looked it too as she stood there with her hands on her hips as if she had all the authority in the world. The gang was more dangerous than it looked. There were six of them, and while they were skinny and dirty, I knew that they were determined. The gangs operated every gate in and out of the First Circle. They took what they wanted and taxed people, unless you were in another gang or had some protection, but that cost you too.

"This baby don't want to pay Daddy. She doesn't want to pay, but she will, won't she?" He winked at me. The rest of them jockeyed around and toadied to him, laughing and nodding with him. "Daddy don't need coin, nope. Daddy takes all forms of payment." He licked his lips and made kissing noises as he circled us. "You know?"

"Uh huh. I do." I punched him squarely in the nose, then yanked his arm behind him and held him as I shoved my knife up under his chin. I didn't shove it through, but I made sure it was piercing him. "Better get back or this daddy gets dead. You know?" The group moved toward us and I pushed the blade up a little more. The leader made pained noises while trying not to open his jaw. "You, greasy fuck, get away from that gate." I nodded at the short guy covered in axel grease operating the gate. He cursed me but scuttled around to join his friends. "Now we're gonna go, and if you move toward us..." I pushed the blade in further and he yelped. The gang yelled and acted as if they were going to come at us, but the leader held up his hand and they held off. "Claire, open the gate." She ran around behind me and struggled to move the heavy metal gate but finally got it open. "Go out. Stay close to the fence." As she went out, I backed up slowly, still holding the idiot. "You're lucky I'm pressed for time." I twisted the blade, and he screamed again. I pulled it free, and as I did, I notched his chin, then shoved him back through the gate. He fell into the dust, howling and screaming as the blood gushed out of his face. I slammed it shut and latched it. The leader jumped up and cursed at us. He motioned for his goons to hit the fence. They all came at the rusty chain link and started bouncing into it and rattling it as they screamed and yelled.

"Fuckers. That noise will bring in every zed for miles, especially any next to the fence." I flipped off the gang, grabbed Claire's arm, and yanked her along. "Move it. We need to get into the trees before any show up looking for dinner."

"But are we even going in the right direction?" Claire asked as we ran for the tree line about fifty yards from the fence.

"Sort of. Just go. Once we're away from this noise, we'll figure it out." She nodded grimly and focused on keeping up as we headed for the wild.

12

A copse of green trees grew in a patch just south of the city. Trees were a blessing and curse. On the one hand, they hid us from watchers and that was needed. We could still hear the shouts from the gang as it ran along the fence line parallel to us, screaming and banging metal against the fence in an attempt to stir up trouble, but we were hidden from them, and soon enough, the path through the little forest took us south and east, which was the direction we needed to go.

I walked slowly and deliberately through the under-brush. Our feet made the leaves and twigs crackle and that was the only noise once we left the sounds of the gang behind. Claire was close behind me. I heard something I didn't like, and I stopped. Claire ran into the back of me.

"What's—"

I held up my hand and cut her off. She knew I was serious and didn't say anything else. I scanned the area. We'd enjoyed the blessing of the cover, but the curse of the trees was that while nobody could see us, we also couldn't see anyone else either. The sound was the slow, regular shuffle of a shambler as it twisted its way through the brambles. I was sure of it, so I pulled out the big blade and waited. Sure enough, once it got a good whiff of us, it moaned and sped up.

It had been a woman. Her calico dress was stained black and worn threadbare. She only had a few wisps of filthy blond hair left; the rest was gone and her scalp covered in rotting sores. Her neck was open; I could see the tendons and sinew inside the ragged bite wound that had killed her. She wasn't crispy, and she wasn't newly dead either, just that rotting middle that they existed in for a weird amount of time. She moaned loudly, tripped over some blackberry brambles, and fell over. None of that stopped her. She dragged herself through the vines and thorns toward us. She reached out for me, but I easily sidestepped her grasp and shoved the blade into her skull. She went slack and collapsed in the brush. I wiped the black blood from my knife on to her dress and looked in the direction from which she came.

"We can't go that way now." I pointed east then north. "Or that direction. I doubt she was wandering out here by herself." The problem was that her direction was precisely the way we needed to go; it was the fastest way to the caravan route and to Sara and Charlie. If I had been by myself, I would have pressed on in that direction. I could be quiet and avoid most anyone. With Claire, I wasn't so sure. In theory, two could keep a lookout better than one, but Claire had never been outside the city. She couldn't climb, she couldn't be quiet enough, and she sure as hell couldn't fight. The weight of her came crashing down on me and I sighed.

I kicked a tree in frustration.

"Leave me," Claire said quietly.

I didn't say anything but the blood all rushed to my head as my adrenaline pumped. It was like she could read my mind, and I was suddenly ashamed.

"No."

"Okay, then talk it through." She pointed to the zed's direction. "You think there are more of them that way, right? But that's the fastest way."

I nodded. "If they're spaced out, okay, I can handle that. If not, and we get bunched up, there's no room to fight or run."

"If you were on your own, you would do it anyway."

"Yep."

"Then do it."

"No. I think we should go south. We'll come out, then skirt the tree line until we find the trail." I started off south, but she grabbed my arm and held me.

"Em, no. It will take too long. I'll just have to fight."

I didn't say anything, but I'm sure the look on my face was transparent to the fact that I didn't believe she could fight. She nodded. "Yes, I can. I have to, right? Do I have any choice? Even if you left me, would I have a choice?"

"No. No matter what, you're going to have to."

She nodded. "Exactly." She looked around. "Can you make me a spear or something?"

That was actually a really good idea, and I was pissed that I hadn't thought of it myself. I found a sturdy branch, cleaned it off, and whittled a sharp point. I handed it to her then made another for myself. She smirked at that but didn't say anything. I couldn't resist. I motioned to the spear. "You shove—"

"Yes, Emily. I get it." She rolled her eyes at me.

"All right, slow. Be as quiet as possible. Watch your feet." I pointed east. "I'm going to try and stay this far apart from you." I was about the length of the stick, maybe four feet away. "Don't get much closer, but if I tell you to stop, maintain the distance."

She nodded. "Okay, let's go."

We started off into the brush. She was much quieter, and I could tell she was watching where she stepped because I could hear slow, deliberate crunches rather than uneven shuffles. I got used to that sound, our sound, and soon that became baseline noise. It made it easier to hear the dead.

We had walked a mile through the tangled under-brush when we heard the moans. I called a stop, and we waited. It didn't take long for three shamblers to crash through the brush and come for us. I took them all out, no issue. It wasn't a problem then but I could hear crashing off in the distance. I shook my head. It was louder, and I could hear multiple moans coming from a few yards out. What was worse was the smell. When zeds got together, there was a distinct smell. If it's a pack of Runners—which it rarely was because they attack anything, even each other—you could smell the piss and shit and body odor. With shamblers, you can smell the overwhelming, sickly sweet smell of rot. When it's a herd, you can smell it for miles. The hot, heavy smell of the rotten horde was suffocating the closer we got to the edge of the trees. We had to take five more out, and when we got to the edge, I stopped and dropped to the ground. Claire did the same.

There was a herd of zeds moving past the tree line. Their moans were low and formed one long hum. Occa-sionally, a few would wander off into the trees, which was why we were seeing the small groups, but mostly they just kept shuffling along through the dead yellow grass—a grotesque parade of rot.

"Fuck," I said. I put my head down on my arms and tried to breathe through my mouth. The smell was over-whelming.

"What do we do? Wait?" Claire asked. She gagged and spit into the leaves.

I shook my head. "We have no idea how big it is. It can take days for them to move through. We don't have time."

"So we go around."

"Which direction? Not north," I whispered. The whole horde of them was moving north, and what was worse was that they were blocking our path to the caravan trail. The thought of the caravan running into this mess made me panic. No way Charlie could deal with it.

"Well, we either go south or back the way we came."

"No. No way. I don't have time for this shit!" I spat into the ground. The light was beginning to fade and it would be dark soon. We couldn't stay there that close to the edge. The shamblers would wander in all night.

"Okay, then we need to decide fast." Claire said. "It's safer back the way we came. Let's go west, just for the night. We'll figure it out in the morning." Claire started to scoot backward.

"Fuck that. I'm not going backward," I said. I looked up. I needed to see what we were dealing with. Maybe the horde wasn't as big or as dense as I thought. Maybe we could use the trick we used before and camouflage ourselves to get through. I needed to see.

I stood up and looked around for the tallest tree I could find. There was a decent sized oak a few yards away with limbs I could reach. It was climbable.

"What are you doing?" Claire asked.

"We need to see how big the horde is. I'm going to take a look." I jumped up, grabbed a thick lower branch, wrapped my legs around it, then pulled myself up.

"We know that south is safe. It's the opposite of them. Let's just go. If you fall, then—"

"Then you can leave me and go wherever the hell you want. I want to know how big it is and if I can squeak through it." I looked down at her. "Stay close to the trunk and keep quiet."

"This is not a good idea," she hissed. "The risk of you hurting yourself is too great."

I shrugged and ignored her, climbing higher. "Everything out here can hurt you. Get used to having no good choices."

She wasn't wrong. It was a decent tree, but I could only go so far, then I would be risking a broken branch and a fall. I had to see, though, so I climbed until the limbs were too spindly to hold me. I latched on to the trunk and the tree groaned and moved with my weight. My foot slipped, and I caught myself. I grasped the trunk tighter and looked out over the plain.

As far as I could see in all three directions, zeds shambled along. The horde was massive, easily the biggest I had ever seen. Thousands. My heart sank. They not only blocked our path, but I had no idea how far east they stretched. Had the caravan outrun them or avoided them? Had they been swallowed by the rotting migration? The zeds were moving north for certain, so Claire was right, south was better. It wasn't at all possible to sneak through them or fight. We had no choice but to go south and try to go around. I just didn't know how long it would take or how far south we'd have to go. There was a limit to how far we could go and that had me worried. We'd cross that bridge when we came to it.

I climbed down as quickly as I could. We didn't have much daylight left.

"South. We go south," I said grimly.

"It's too big," she said.

"Way too big," I said. "We're going to go back a bit to get away from them, then head south along the tree line. We need to find a place to stop for the night."

"Stop? Where would we stop?" Claire asked as we walked west for a few hundred yards, then turned south, parallel to the horde.

"Wherever we can," I said. "We can't see in the dark. Not to walk and not to fight."

"But, there's nothing out here. What if—" Claire looked nervous, and she scanned the tree line to our left.

"Welcome to life. Yeah. They can get to us. So can a thousand and one other terrible things." We walked about an hour in silence as she digested that. I mean, I didn't know what else to tell her. This was just everyday life for everyone except her kind.

I stopped when I found a small clearing. There was room to maneuver and a fire space with charcoal and stuff littered around. It was obvious that people camped here frequently. That was good and bad. I didn't want company of any kind, living or dead, but this was better than hunkering down in underbrush all night.

"No fire, right?" Claire asked. She looked around suspiciously.

"Definitely not," I said. "It isn't cold and the light will draw them in. It will draw all sorts of things in."

She nodded. "What should I do?"

"Rest. Nothing else to do. I'm going to watch for a while. I'll wake you up when I need a break." I sat down in the dirt next to the fire pit. There were bones and trash littering the area. I hated looking at bones. You always found more than you wanted to find when you poked around an old fire. Some of the bones were animal, but some weren't. The ones around this fire were mixed, and that made me nervous. Claire picked it up too. I guess I should have expected that with her background.

"Emily, these are human."

"Yep."

"We're not safe here."

"We're not safe anywhere."

"How can you be so casual about this?" She seemed to settle, but she was twitchy and she kept looking around. We could still hear the moans of the herd off in the distance. The forest was dead quiet. No animals, no birds. Nothing alive but us as everything else had sense enough to get as far away as possible.

"I can't change it. It's just how it is," I said. "No use in getting excited about it."

"Who even lives out here? Why don't they live in the cities?"

"Like the Circles are safe? You have to be three in before you can sleep, and besides, some people like this. No rules. If I didn't have Sara, I'd probably still be out here."

She scooted a bit closer to me but didn't lie down.

"You lived out here?"

"Since the beginning. We scavenged." I pulled my knees up to my chest. My parents kept us together for as long as they could. It couldn't have been easy. I was a toddler. Charlie, useless. Danny was fifteen, and he had taken to the new world like a duck to water. I didn't remember my dad—he died when I was four—Danny was a dad and a brother and a best friend. He taught me everything and somehow managed to keep us going as a family. When my mom died, he got us going and made all three of us promise to take care of each other. He was firm and gentle with me. He was patient and kind to Charlie. I wanted to be exactly like him. Brave. Smart. Tough. I always felt like I only got one out of three.

"Do you remember anything from before?" she asked.

"No. I was two." I heard something crash through the growth and a shambler popped through. I got up and took care of it, then dragged it off as far as possible. It stunk. I sat back down.

"I was older. I remember many things. The world wasn't like this," Claire said. She smiled, but seemed sad. "I remember school and birthday parties. Parks. Playing."

"Kids still play," I said. "But it's tough to be out here and survive. Not like it's easy anywhere but, you know. Although right now, I'll take this over the city and all that. At least I can see what's coming at me out here."

"Yes. I suppose you could look at it that way." She began to relax a little. I knew she was exhausted. "It could be different. We could make it better."

I laughed. "How? How could we make this better? People have tried to bring it back. The disease is too good. And people are just not."

"There are plenty of good people," Claire said.

"Really? I've met very few of them." I laughed.

"You're a good person." She smiled at me. I rolled my eyes.

"I'm not."

"You could leave me. You could do it now or in the

morning. It's what you should do if you want to find your family quickly, but you won't."

"You're right. That's exactly what I should do," I said. "In the morning."

She laughed this time. "You won't. It's not in you to do it."

"You don't know me. I've done much worse than just leave you."

"I doubt it," she said. "And whatever you did, you did to help somebody else. Your brother. Sara."

"Shut up and go to sleep."

"I should leave you. Save you the trouble," she whispered as she laid her head down on her arms.

"That would be great, but do it later. I'll need some sleep tonight too." I kept scanning the clearing. If she left, it would save me some trouble. I could go faster. I wouldn't worry about anyone else. She wouldn't get in my way. But I had a funny feeling at the thought of her leaving me. It scared me a little, like the thought of Danny leaving had, only not nearly as bad, just a shadow of it, but it was familiar and unpleasant. "I'll wake you up in a couple of hours."

"Ok," she said, then she stilled. I knew she wasn't asleep. She was lying there, thinking about what to do next, just like in a few hours, I wouldn't be able to sleep either.

13

She hadn't left during the night. I hadn't been able to sleep either, but it felt okay just to rest. We had no food and no water, and we needed both, so as soon as the sun started to rise, we were on our way. We moved parallel to the horde, and after a few hours we came to the southern edge of the forest. I paused and looked out of the trees.

The horde wasn't past. Not even close to past.

"Do you think we can wait them out?" Claire asked.

I shook my head. "Nope. It could take days for all of them to go by. We need water, like today or we'll end up shuffling along with them."

"What do we do?"

"I don't know," I said.

"Do you know where you are? Have you been here before?" Claire asked.

I looked out over the plain where the horde was shuffling through. I did know where I was. Danny and Charlie and I had come this way a lot, but we usually didn't go west from here. West from here wasn't really anywhere you ever wanted to be, although to be fair, no place out here was exactly where you wanted to be.

"I know where we are. That doesn't change this." I motioned to the parade of corpses in front of us.

"So, you know where we are, but what we don't know is how many more of them there are, right?" Claire motioned out to the herd, then up at a tree. "We find out."

I looked up at the tree she was looking at. It was a spindly pine. I looked at her. "I can't climb that one."

She nodded. "No, but I can." She was slight—much slighter than I was, for sure—but she couldn't climb.

"You? Not likely."

"I can do it. You definitely can't. Boost me up." She moved over to the tree. The first limb was seven feet off the ground.

I put my hands down to lift her up. "If you fall—"

"It's the same as if you fall. Calculated risk, Emily."

She put her foot in my hands and grabbed my shoulders. I lifted her up, and she grabbed the limb. It was shiny and sticky with sap, which was likely going to help her. She scrambled around, but she finally pulled herself up. I stood underneath, ready to catch her if she fell, but that was probably dumb. We both didn't need to get hurt.

It took her a while—she was annoyingly slow at climbing—but she did it. Her small frame allowed her to go quite a bit higher than I had been able to climb in the other tree. She stayed up there a good while. Finally she came down. She slipped a few times, and when I finally got her on the ground, she was tired. Her arms and legs shook from the effort and she was winded and flushed.

"It's the tail end of them, I think. They're not densely packed and they're sporadic. Also, I can see some kind of fence in the distance. I can't tell how far though, but honestly, I think we could make it there."

"Yeah. I know what that fence is. It's not exactly safety."

"Well, it's safer than a group of infected." Claire tried to wipe the sap off her hands. She finally rubbed them in the dirt.

"If you knew what was behind that fence you might think differently," I said. "We still have to get past the zeds."

"We need a distraction."

I looked around. We had scrub brush and dead leaves. I pulled out the lighter we took off the Handler. "This is a terrible idea," I said.

Claire started bunching up leaves and piling brush and limbs. When we had three big piles spaced out down the tree line, I had her wait at the southern edge of the trees and I lit the piles. When each was burning well, I calmly walked down to the edge and joined her.

"Should we run now?" Claire asked. She began to cough a bit as smoke filled the area.

"Wait. Let them go to the fires." I pointed toward the zeds, which had spotted the lights and were starting to moan and turn in that direction. We waited. She was nervous. I could tell she really wanted to run. I did too, but we had to wait until we got a solid contingent moving and an edge opened up. We could hear them all crashing into the undergrowth toward the fires. Finally, we could see the edge of them, and I saw the fence Claire had seen. It was a few hundred yards away. Not a big deal to run normally, not when I didn't have a bum ankle and not if I had been by myself. But I wasn't by myself and I did have a bad ankle, so I was looking for our best shot.

"When I say go, just jog, slow and easy. Don't make any sudden movements to draw their attention. Go for the fence and start climbing. I'll be right behind you." I pulled the big knife out and got ready to run. This was bad odds. I saw twenty-five shamblers at least between the fence and us. But honestly, it helped to think of it that way, like a match in the Arena. I had a blade. I had a distraction. It was doable. If I did one last thing.

I nodded at Claire. "Ok, go." She took off at a steady jog which was impressive because I could tell from her white face and pursed lips that she was terrified. She kept a decent distance from the stragglers of the herd and she was about a quarter of the way to the fence when I started screaming. I jumped in the brush and banged on the trees until there was no doubt that any of the zeds that might have gone for her were now coming for me.

Good and bad. Good because at halfway, she had started to lose steam. She wasn't a runner. Hadn't been from day one and I knew no way was she going to make it all the way to the fence unless I got them coming to me. It worked well, if that's even the best way to describe it, and I gritted my teeth and started running myself. I kept steady, but I stopped every little while to take one out and yell for the rest. Claire stopped when she heard me yelling, and was pissed when she saw what I had done, but I could tell she knew why because she shook her head and concentrated on running faster.

The zeds were close, grabbing for me and doing their best, but I can say with no ego— okay very little ego— that this was what I did, what I was designed to do. When a thing does exactly what it's designed to do, it's something beautiful. Zeds were steadily piling around me as I casually jogged through the remains of the herd. I stopped every little bit and yelled when one got too close to Claire. She dodged them pretty well, but she was tired. She slowed so much that I finally caught up with her when we were ten yards from the fence.

"Just a little more," I said as I shoved the blade into the skull of a crispy zed. He looked like he'd been burned; his face was charred and black. "Go on, get to the fence and start climbing." I pushed her forward.

She stumbled up against the fence and tried to climb, but it looked like she was out of gas. While most of the herd had started for the fires, a decent group—more than I could handle alone—followed us to the fence.

"Look, I know you're tired but you need to climb. Get your ass up and over that fence now." I took two more out as she climbed. She was slow, only about six feet up the fence. I couldn't wait any longer myself. I kept them off until she was mostly out of reach, holstered my knife, and climbed.

I passed her in no time and was sitting on top of the fence while she was still climbing. "Come on," I said as I straddled the top and held out my hand. "Claire, hurry the fuck up or you're going to join their party." Her foot slipped, and she yelled. Somehow, she held on as the zeds below moaned and grabbed for her. "Don't think about them. Don't look at them." I calmed my voice and remembered a time when Danny had been in my position and a seven-year-old me had been where Claire was now. He sat atop of the fence calmly and made me focus and climb. He was good like that, always calm and collected, even when shit had gone as south as it could go. Charlie would be scrambling, huffing and screaming, but Danny was chill and in control, always. I never remembered him being anything else, not even at the end. I closed my eyes and exhaled as I thought of him.

"Hey. Claire. You're fine. You climbed that tree, right? This is much easier. Focus. Only a little more to go. Look up. Look at me. Come on. Just a little more to go, then you can take my hand." I held my hand down to her. She looked like she was about to cry and let go. I could see her arms shaking. Her hands clawed desperately into the wire of the fence.

"Claire. Don't you fucking dare let go. Do you hear me? You're not going to fall. I won't let you. So put your foot in the next hole and push. Come on. Do it."

She looked up at me, then down at the zeds below and she paused for a second. She raised her head and cried, but she climbed far enough up for me to grab her hand. I gripped it tightly and hauled her up. Once we got up and over, we started to climb down. I went quickly, avoiding the zeds that clawed at us through the fence. She wasn't so lucky. They grabbed at her feet and she freaked out and lost her grip. I was under her, trying to clear a few out with my knife, and she fell right on top of me.

"Em, are you ok?" she asked.

"I guess. I'd be better if you got off me," I said. She scrambled around awkwardly and got up. She was still shaking.

"What is this place? Why is it fenced?"

I stood up, checked everything, and dusted myself off. "It's a junk yard."

"So it belongs to salvagers?"

"It belongs to *a* salvager, and if we're very lucky, we'll never see him," I said. I looked around. There was metal everywhere—junk cars, scraps, old appliances, coils of wire, I-beams, rebar, just garbage, and tons of it. Danny had sold here on occasion, but it was always a last resort.

"I don't understand," Claire said. "Maybe he can help us."

I shook my head. "We have nothing of value. He won't help us. As I said, if we're fortunate, we'll make it to the other side of the salvage yard before he even knows we're here. Stay quiet, keep moving, and watch out for zeds. He lets runners loose in here, like guard dogs, only nastier."

She frowned. "That's barbaric. Who is this person?"

I made sure we had all our stuff and that the fence was holding, then I turned cautiously west. "Barbaric, yeah, that's him all right." I began to pick our way through the maze of garbage hoping that I never had to see him or speak his name again.

We picked our way slowly through the maze of junk and trash. At first I tried to stick to the outside as close to the fence line as possible. I knew that the center of the salvage yard was no place I wanted to be, but unfortunately, the edges around the fence were blocked by scrap metal, wooden pallets, and big junk that prevented anyone from doing exactly what I wanted to do, which was stick to the edge and go unnoticed.

We wound back and forth in circles, and it didn't take Claire long to figure out what was happening.

"We're being directed. Funneled," she said.

"Yes. Into a trap." I stopped walking. The corridor of trash and junk was twenty feet tall. We couldn't see anything. There was an opening about ten feet ahead and it looked like a clearing in the junk. I shook my head. No good could come of it. That was definitely not where we wanted to be.

I heard squeaking and screeching all around us as rats fought and scurried about.

Claire looked around, disgusted. "Rats?"

"Rats," I confirmed.

"It's a garbage dump," she said as if the rats needed to be justified.

"It's more like a death trap," I said. "Stay quiet. I don't like what's ahead." I nodded toward the opening.

She stood still and pulled out one of the batons. I was impressed. She was learning.

I walked slowly toward the opening and flattened against the wall of trash. I felt squirming behind me and heard screeching. I swallowed down my disgust and waited for them to quiet. Once they did, I heard intense growling and snarling. I could also hear sobbing. I peeked out into the clearing.

Three runners jumped and stalked beneath a cage hanging in the clearing. They screeched and snarled as they reached for a girl in the cage. The girl was naked and filthy, balled up in a fetal position in the small cage. The runners couldn't get to her, and they were angry. They spit and screamed in frustration. If they jumped, they could just brush the bottom of the cage with their fingers.

The cage swayed and creaked every time they touched it. The girl didn't move, she just sobbed.

He loved it. I knew he did, and I knew he was somewhere watching. You didn't see him, but he liked his entertainment. I knew we'd have to cross the clearing to get out, or at least to move on to whatever else was in the way. Three runners were a challenge. All at once, I'd be in trouble. We would need to use the trash to help us out. I got a good grip on my knife and motioned for Claire. "Three runners. I'll get them. Be ready if I don't. Run back the way we came and go for the fence," I whispered. "Give me the other baton." I held out my hand, and she gave it to me. "When I say so, start banging around on this crap." I pointed to the metal all around us.

"That's going to bring them right to us," she whispered fiercely. "I don't think that's a good idea—"

"It's all I got. I'll take them out, but I want them one on one. The trash will funnel them to us."

It wasn't great, I had to admit, but I knew if I went out there alone, they would rush me and we would be done.

"Ok, I'm ready," she said. She grabbed the baton in a two-handed grip and found a piece of metal.

I went to the edge of the opening and waited. I looked back and nodded at her. She started wailing on a metal car fender for all she was worth. I heard the zeds scream and growl. The sounds got closer, as did the smell of shit and piss. When the first one popped her head in the opening at us, I bashed her with the baton. She dropped to the ground and convulsed. I shoved the blade into her eye and she quit twitching. I didn't have to wait long until the second one rushed in. He got all the way in before I hit him in the side of the face. He didn't go down right away. He had been moving away from my blow and it just glanced him. He grabbed for me and clawed, but I hit his arm and heard it crack. He screamed and pulled it back, and while he did that, the third one came barreling into the opening, screaming and spitting.

I ignored the one with the broken arm and focused on the third. She was livid mad and determined as she spit black foam everywhere. She made a funny excited chittering noise, like a cat when it sees a bird it wants to kill it, and she pounced. I sidestepped her, and she crashed into the garbage wall, sending rats running everywhere. One ran right over my head and jumped at the zed. She went insane as she caught it and ate it. As she ripped it apart, I got up and bashed her in the head. She just screamed at me so I bashed her two or three more times until she fell down.

Claire was swiping at the zed with the busted arm but she wasn't making solid contact. I came up behind him and jammed the knife into his kidneys. He fell to his knees, and I reached around him and slit his throat. He gurgled and fell over. I shoved the knife into the base of his skull to finish it so he wouldn't come back, and did the same with the other one.

"That wasn't as bad as I thought it would be," Claire said, out of breath.

"That was the easy part," I said. I wiped my knife on the dead guy and went to the edge of the trash. I looked out at the girl in the cage. She was still sobbing despite the zeds being gone, so I assumed she was broken. She'd be no help.

Claire came up beside me and looked out. "Em, we have to help her."

"There's no helping her," I said.

"Of course there is, she's alive. We can't leave her."

"That's exactly what we're going to do. She's mental. Look at her." I motioned around the clearing. "And there are traps out there somewhere. She's bait."

"We're not leaving her in that cage," she said with finality.

"We do not have time for this," I said, but she wasn't going to argue.

"If that was Sara in that cage, would you want somebody to have time to help her?"

I glared at her. "Don't fucking ever play that shit with me again." I poked her in the chest with the baton. "Don't fucking touch anything and stay behind me. Don't walk anywhere I haven't."

"Wouldn't the infected have set off any traps?"

It was a fair point, and I ignored it. "Just shut up and do what I tell you. We're not taking her with us."

"I'll help her," Claire said.

"Oh, sure, okay," I laughed meanly.

"Just go, Emily," she said.

I walked slowly into the clearing. The cage hung from a wooden pillar. The thick nylon rope looked new. She hadn't been hanging that long, or at least not with that rig. I traced the rope back to the pillar and saw where it was tied off. I didn't see anything that looked like a snare or pressure switch around it, but I stepped carefully anyway. I unwound the rope and let her down easy. She didn't move or acknowledge me in any way. She was either really mental or in on it.

We looked at the closure on the cage. It was just zip tied shut. I cut it with my knife and the cage swung open. The girl was disgusting. She had shit all over herself and she was covered in sores. I could see every bone in her spine and her cheeks were angular and hollow. I was not digging touching her, not because she was filthy, but because she could have been infected. She wasn't responding at all.

Claire leaned down to her. "Hey, you're free. Come on, we're here to help."

"No. No. Put me back," the girl sobbed.

"Why would you want to go back? You're safe now," Claire put a hand on the girl's black, crusted back.

The girl shrieked and shied away further into the cage. "It's safer here. Better than what comes next," she sobbed.

"No, it can't be. Come on, we're getting out of here." Claire patted her.

The girl stopped sobbing and looked up at us. Her eyes were wild, fierce blue in a field of black filth. She began to laugh hysterically. "You're never getting out of here." She laughed louder and louder and reached out and shut the door of the cage.

"She's bonkers. Let's go Claire."

"She's not rational at all. Who did this to her?" Claire looked around angrily.

"We did it!" A voice boomed. We didn't see anyone, but I did see a speaker on a pole. I knew he was watching.

Claire stood defiantly. "You can't treat people like this."

"We can do whatever we want," the voice laughed.

"Claire, don't argue with him. Let's just get out of here." I grabbed her arm and started dragging her along toward one of the openings opposite from the one we'd come in.

"Are you sure that's the right way, Emily?" The voice said.

"Does he know you?" Claire asked as she looked around, still angry.

"Oh yes. He knows me," I said.

"Let me guess, you didn't part on the best of terms?"

"Claire, does it really seem like it would matter to him if we did?" I motioned around. "Move."

"That way could be out or it could be not out," the voice laughed. "Emily always thinks she knows, but we know, don't we?"

I chose the path to the left. None of them led out. They all led to terrible shit. I held my hand up and flipped him off as we started down the trash corridor.

He laughed louder. The echoes of his laughter reverberated through the trash and followed us as we walked.

15

"How do you know we're going toward the exit?" Claire asked as we wound through the garbage. I kicked a huge, fat rat that stood up on its hind legs and hissed at us.

"None of the paths lead to the exit," I said grimly.

"One has to," she said. She sidestepped the big rat which was groggy from his flight but still irate.

"No, it doesn't. He won't let us just walk out of here. This path leads to a trap or some other shitty situation that he wants to see if we can survive."

"So, we should never have climbed the fence," she said.

"We shouldn't have come this far south. For sure."

"Who is this person?"

"He's the Rat King. Scavenger. You can buy stuff and

sell your scavenge here if you can stomach him." We were coming to an opening again. I stopped and listened. I couldn't hear any growling or moans, but there had to be something out there.

"The Rat King?"

"He's a sadistic old fuck, and he likes rats." I shrugged. "It's what he calls himself."

"And you know him well, because…"

"Scavenging is what we did when Danny was alive, before Charlie got hurt." I peeked out. The space was another tunnel with high walls of junk. The path was open and clear, which was a bad sign. It was a funnel of some sort. I looked at the sides of the walls. I wondered if we could climb on them and avoid the ground.

"And you sold to him?" Claire looked disgusted.

"We sold to everyone," I said. "We couldn't afford to be choosey about business associates."

"I didn't mean to imply—"

"You did mean to. This isn't the world you think it is, Claire. Good people have to do bad stuff sometimes." I pointed to the walls. "I think we need to avoid the ground."

"How does he get captives?" she asked.

"Traps them. Double-crosses them. Buys them." I knelt down and looked at the ground on its level. "Okay, I'm going to climb. Going to try it."

"Buys?"

"Yep. Happens all the time out here."

She was livid. Her face got red, and she sputtered. "That's the most repellent thing I've heard. Did you—"

I looked at her and shook my head. "Hey, how about getting pissed about it after we get out of here?"

"Did you?"

"What if I did? What if I needed the money so as not to starve? What if I needed it for medicine for my bother? What if I only sold him bad people?"

"You didn't." She looked relieved.

"I've never given this miserable freak anything and I never would. He chopped off Charlie's leg, and he's a double-crossing piece of shit. You deal with him long enough and he will get you. Now can we please get out of here?"

She nodded. "I don't know if I can climb."

"Well, I'm like ninety percent sure that whole trail is booby trapped." I pointed to the dirt path. "So climb."

I started scaling the side wall. There was plenty to hold on to: hunks of concrete, junk, rebar. I had no trouble at all. The only issues were the rats that poked out constantly and bit me. I'd be lucky not to get sick from them, but a few rat bites were better than whatever he had laid out on the pathway. Claire was behind me and even she could climb it, it was so easy. Too easy.

He wanted us to do it. Why? Maybe there were no traps on the path. Maybe climbing was the trap, and we had gone right along with it. One thing I did know was that he was always going to be a trap ahead of us. This was his world. He knew it and we didn't.

"Claire. I'm going to need you to trust me."

She stopped moving and looked at me, confused. "I do. What are you thinking?"

"This whole place is a trap. We'll never beat him this way."

"We have to change the rules," she said. "Okay, what do you want to do?"

"I want to spring his trap." I pointed to a suspect handhold just above me. "I'll get caught. When I do, you hide. Follow him."

"No," she said. "It can't be you. I'll do it."

"I might be able to get him when he gets close," I said.

"I don't think he'll be that careless with you. He knows you. He doesn't know me. I'll be easier to manage." She started to climb around me. "We'll make like you want me around you because we're almost through." When she got to the other side of me, she looked at me. "If you get a chance to leave me and find Charlie and Sara, you do it."

"Not happening," I said. "We're both getting out of here."

"I hope so," she said as she reached up and pulled the lever. A mountain of trash and rats came loose as she fell. When she hit the ground, a pressure switch triggered, and a net closed around her. I dug down deep inside the trash and hid. I squashed a few rats and waited. We didn't have to wait long. After only a few minutes, he came swaggering into view.

He was every bit as disgusting as I remembered. Covered in black grime, the only thing white on him were his eyeballs and his teeth. His hair was long and stringy and his face pointed and rodential, just like the denizens of his shit kingdom. He laughed at Claire as she struggled in the heavy cargo net. He looked around for me and smiled when he couldn't find me. "She left you, pretty."

Claire stopped struggling and glared at him. "I think you're going to regret this."

"We think you are going to regret it, too," he said. I winced as he reached out and rapped her on the head with a small club. It knocked her out, and she slumped on the ground. He picked her up, net and all, then began whistling as he carried her out, back the way we had come. I dug myself out of the trash and followed silently.

He wound around through the trash and I thought I lost him once or twice, but I was able to follow his trail. It led back to a familiar place. The Rat King was nothing if not theatrical. He had made a mini-amphitheater in the trash. He wasn't alone. There were four other people in various restraints in the amphitheater. One skinny blonde boy was staked to a cross on wheels. There were three girls crammed into small cages meant for a medium-sized dog. They were filthy and moaned constantly. He deposited Claire in an open kennel and padlocked it closed. She was, groggy, but still mad.

I settled in to watch. I noticed the key ring on his belt. I knew he kept a big key that opened the front gate where he traded. It was closest to the caravan trail, and that's where we wanted to go. A well-worn, much neater path led out of the other side of the amphitheater. It had to be the way out.

Claire banged on the cage door. She noticed the padlock and shook her head. It was up to me and she knew it. I watched her look around. She was looking for me. He noticed.

"We've shown her where the exit is. If we know Emily, she is headed there now," he said. He beat on Claire's cage with a small pipe. "Have you met everyone?" He pointed to the three girls. "Stacey, Casey, and Tracey. You already met Tracey. She's been with us quite a while. Lots of fun, she is." The girl lay still and cried. "And that's Chris, there on the cross. Chris doesn't speak much. He doesn't have a tongue any longer." The Rat King bent down and smiled at Claire. "What is your name?" He asked.

"I wouldn't give you the satisfaction of knowing," Claire replied.

"Nice to meet you, Gail." He bowed and laughed.

He was right. I could find my way out. And I didn't

need the key to the front gate. I could climb it. I thought about it. He wouldn't kill Claire right away. He would keep her alive for a while. I just needed a few days to find Charlie and Sara. Once they were safe, I'd come back for Claire.

Only that wasn't what I said I was going to do. I knew if I did it, she wouldn't hate me. She'd understand, but I'd asked her if she trusted me. She didn't hesitate with her answer.

The Rat King hummed a happy tune as he went to work. He opened Tracey's cage and yanked her out by her hair. She didn't fight him, she just whimpered. She was so skinny and filthy that I doubted she could protest much. He dragged her over to a brown stained piece of plywood. There were big rings attached to it at the four corners and he zip-tied her wrists and ankles to the rings. He had a boom arm on a swivel with a come-a-long attached. The plywood had a chain attached. He hooked through the chain to the come-a-long, then used a hand winch to suspend the plywood upright. He dragged Claire's cage over close to another piece of plywood. I knew he'd have a much tougher time getting Claire to be as compliant as the other girl. He didn't open her cage. He just knelt and smiled.

"Gail, since you're new we want you to have a special view of the floor show." He pulled the other plywood back to reveal a pit. I knew what was going to happen next. The walls of the pit were pocked with holes of various sizes. He maneuvered the boom arm so that the plywood with Tracey staked out on it was over the open pit. He then used the winch again and slowly lowered the screaming girl into the pit. And I mean, she screamed for all she was worth. She was hysterical, and for the first time, she actually tried to get out of the restraints. She knew what was coming.

I watched Claire stare down into the pit. She didn't recognize the holes, but the screaming girl was enough to upset her. "Whatever you're going to do, stop it now." Claire used that same authoritative voice she had used with the guards. The Rat King was unimpressed.

"Us? We're not going to do anything," he laughed.

The squeaking was low, but as the sleek, fat, rats emerged from their holes, the squeaking got louder and more excited.

"Did you know rats like human flesh? They love it actually. Prefer to anything else." He sat crossed-legged beside Claire's cage and watched alongside her. "We can throw all sorts of things in there. Cats, dogs, a goat. They'll sometimes eat and sometimes, they turn their nose up." He pointed to the shrieking Tracey, whose screams weren't having much effect on the advancing rats. "But when we put a person in there, they all come out and they are so excited." He clapped and laughed. The rats scattered at the sudden noise, but they came back a few seconds later. He laughed and pointed to a huge fat rat. It squeezed out of its hole and waddled confidently up to the girl. It hissed, then bit into her savagely. The rest followed, and Tracey's panicked screams turned into miserable wails as the rats ate her.

He looked around, probably for me. "You know, we think Emily really did head for the exit. We wouldn't have thought she would stand by and let the babies have anyone."

Claire looked horrified. She stared down into the pit. "You're going to be very sorry that you did this," she said quietly.

"We doubt that very much, Gail. We think Emily is gone, but let's find out." He raised the plywood out of the hole. The rats were indignant. They were still eating and Tracey wasn't dead. They clung to her and bit even harder. He laughed at them. "You're all so silly." There wasn't anything silly about them. They were vicious. When he set the plywood down, he lowered it all the way and some of the rats scurried back into the pit, but some —the big nasty one—screamed loudly in protest, but kept eating.

He unhooked the plywood and pulled the boom arm over to Claire's cage. He latched the hook to the top of her cage, raised it off the ground, then maneuvered it over the pit.

"They might take longer than normal because they

snacked on Tracey, but they'll finish you, eventually." He stood by the winch, ready to lower her.

I stepped out from where I had been hiding. He clapped delightedly and smiled.

"Emily! We thought you had left, didn't we Gail?" He held his arms out wide as if he wanted a hug.

I walked purposefully toward him and when he opened up, I threw my knife right at him. It lodged in his stomach. He stared at it a second, then hit the lever on the winch, sending Claire in her cage crashing into the pit. The rats screeched and so did Claire. I kept after him though. When I got to him, he was crawling away. I pulled him by his leg and whacked him a couple of times with my baton. He scooted back against the garbage wall.

"Better get Gail out of the pit. The babies will have her," he said.

"Not all of her." I punched him a couple of times until he was unconscious. "Idiot."

I ran over to the pit. Claire was okay. She bashed at rats with her hands as they tried to come in the cage. The hook had detached so I couldn't pull her out. I'd have to hook it back up to get her. I looked down at the rats and grimaced. They made my skin crawl.

"Emily—" Claire screamed.

"Yeah, I know. I'm coming," I said with an exasperated sigh. I grabbed the hook and made sure I had enough slack, then I took a deep breath before jumping down into the pit.

I kicked a bunch of rats out of the way but they were bold and kept after my legs. I bashed all around the cage with my club. Some blows sent the little bastards running, and some just seemed to enrage them. They were kind of like zeds, only with the instinct of self-preservation. I hooked the chain to the cage then climbed out of the pit, using the rat holes as holds.

When I pulled her out, she was yelling at the rats, and some were still clinging to the cage. I moved the boom arm over and set her down, then whacked the rest of the rats off the cage. Claire was shaking.

"Em, get me out of here."

"Working on it," I said. I grabbed the key ring from the Rat King and found the correct key. Claire crawled out of the cage. She had lots of little bloody spots where the rats bit her, but she was mostly fine.

I unlocked the other two cages. The naked girls looked stunned, and they just sat there, cowering. Claire tried talking to them, but she gave up. They just stared at her blankly and rocked. I got the kid off the cross and he took off into the junkyard without saying anything.

We stood over the Rat King. He had zip ties in his pockets, which I used to tie his wrists and ankles. He groaned and mumbled, then opened his eyes. He blinked a few times before trying to move. When he couldn't, he looked down at his hands and feet He grinned at me.

"So wonderful to see you again. You'll never get out, you know. Only we know the way."

"You're so full of shit, Ralph," I said. "That path right there leads back to your trailer and the front."

"Perhaps," he said. "What do you plan on doing? We'll get free, you know."

"I agree with you there. You will wiggle out of this eventually if I let you." The wound in his stomach was bleeding, but not gushing. It wouldn't kill him.

"What are you going to do?" Claire asked.

"Me? I'm not going to do anything," I said.

Both he and Claire understood.

"No, Emily. No," he said. "We'll pay you. What do you want? How much do you want?"

"Can you give Charlie back his leg?" I asked.

Claire looked surprised.

"Yeah. He fed Charlie's leg to the rats," I said. "That really set us back, Ralph."

"We're sorry. Come on, that was a long time ago. And look at you now. Famous."

"No more talk." I dragged him to the pit and shoved him in. He screamed and cursed at me. I ignored him as I slid the plywood covers back over top of the pit.

"Seems cruel," Claire said. We listened to him scream

when the squeaking and screeching started. It was muffled, but we could still hear it.

"Seems like justice to me," I said. "He'll never do that to anyone else."

"No, I suppose you're right about that."

"I was never going to leave you with him," I said.

"I know. That would have been in your best interest. You never do what's in your best interest."

"Sometimes I do."

"You don't actually, but you'd better start soon. How do we get out of here?"

"Probably that way," I said as I pointed toward the pathway.

"So you really didn't know?" She looked annoyed at me. "He could have led us out."

"He'd have led us into another trap. Besides, we can figure it out. He'll have water and supplies somewhere and maybe a vehicle."

"Maybe it wasn't a bad thing coming here then." Claire started down the path.

"Oh no, it was. We got lucky," I said as I followed her. We were cautious, but after a while, I realized he kept this path neater and groomed. His trailer was well stocked with food, water, and other supplies. We drank and ate and decided to stay the night. It was safe there, and we both needed the rest. We settled in on the floor of the trailer. It was disgusting and stunk like body odor and rat piss, but I'd slept in worse.

"You get lucky a lot," Claire said. She yawned and stretched out on the floor.

"Not as often as I'd like," I replied.

16

The morning brought us a renewed sense of hope. We had a few supplies. I found a couple of backpacks that Ralph had likely taken off some unlucky traveler and loaded up on food and water. I couldn't find any vehicles except the big equipment that he used to move trash around, but that was okay. He was flush with supplies. He not only had the income from the salvage yard, but he'd been trapping people and taking their stuff for years. We took what we needed, and I kept his key ring. I had plans for the salvage yard someday. It would be safer for Sara, and Charlie could run it now that Ralph was out of the picture. I laughed a little because for the first time in a long time I felt like I had a long-term plan.

Danny had been better at that stuff. Charlie was

terrible at planning of any sort, and I was better in a pinch, not with the desired future state stuff. Danny always kept us moving toward the future and he always saw a better one. I only ever saw the immediate slog, the fight. Thinking about what could be felt kind of good for once. I locked the gate behind us and pocketed the keys.

"What about the others inside?" Claire asked.

"They can climb out or not. They aren't my concern."

"I feel bad that we couldn't help them." Claire shouldered her pack and set off next to me. She could have stayed there. It would have been safer for her and I could have moved faster, but something told me I might need her later, so I didn't suggest that she stay and she didn't bring it up, either. I thought maybe she might have been afraid to stay there by herself, but knowing her as I did, I think she thought she needed to stick with me too.

"Don't. We saved their lives. What they do next is on them." I pointed to north. "We should be able to pick up the trail in a mile or so. I couldn't see anything over the flat plain, but I could see hills in the distance and the caravan trail ran between us and the big hills, right next to the river.

"I suppose so. It just feels like we should help them more."

"They wouldn't have helped us. Notice the kid didn't stick around. He might have been feral. Or maybe he's feral now. I don't know."

"You don't know that they wouldn't have helped us. They were all traumatized." Claire rolled her eyes at me. "You think the worst of everyone."

"That's because everyone is basically the worst," I said. "You need to wise up. Things out here are not fair. No control at all. If you think anyone is going to do anything other than look out for themselves, you are going to be unhappily surprised."

"I'm not operating like that. You don't do that."

"I do. Out here is different," I said.

"You almost never operate in your own best interest. If you did, you would have left me back in the Arena."

"You're somewhat useful. I was planning ahead." We walked and finally found the caravan trail. It was easy enough to find. The heavy-laden wagon wheels cut deep grooves into the ground, and the big draft horses left hoof prints and piles of shit.

"How do you know they're the right caravan?" Claire asked.

"Doesn't matter. They stack up on this trail. They might be the next one in line or they might be two up. We'll find them." I looked around cautiously. The trail would be easy to follow and there was almost always traffic, which was good and bad. Good because it was simple. Bad because people were almost always a bad idea out here. Claire was clueless about it, but people were wild and different out here. We could run into simple travelers, scavengers, bandits, or people who defied description, if you could even call them people. I had always found it a best practice to keep my distance. Joining up with groups invited trouble. It attracted zeds. Pick the wrong traveling companion and you might end up in a cage, entertainment for the Rat King or worse.

"Ok, listen. On the trail, we're going to see groups. Don't stop." We started off down the trail, skirting the tree line by the river. I wanted options in case things got hot, and the trees might be of help.

"I get that we're in a hurry Emily," she said.

"We are in a hurry, but groups and camps are trouble. You need to listen and trust me. Follow my lead."

"I'll do my best," she said.

We walked a few miles as quickly as I could without running. We were going to have a hard time catching that caravan at our pace. My hope was that we would overtake them, but I was also prepared if we had to go all the way to Piney Bottom, the next settlement out. Charlie would wait there as long as he could.

It was mid-day, and it was hot. I was wet with sweat and Claire was soaked and red in the face.

"Can we stop a minute?" she asked, her breath slightly lost. I forgot she was hauling a pack too.

"Yeah, for a minute," I said. I sat down on the ground and opened my bag. I drank a bottle of water and ate an apple. Claire did the same.

"How long do you think it will take to catch up to them?"

"I don't know. They had a couple of days head start already and we got delayed a few days more. Worst case is we catch them in Piney Bottom." I knew perfectly well that wasn't the worst case. The trail was dangerous and the caravan they were traveling with was shady at best.

"Isn't Piney Bottom, umm, questionable?" She finished her lunch.

"Everywhere is questionable," I said. "I guess I wouldn't pick Piney Bottom out to raise a family, yeah."

"Can your brother handle himself?"

"Probably not." I said. I got up and filled our water bottles from the river.

Charlie should have been able to handle it. He had been to Piney Bottom as much as me, but he was just useless at most everything. My mom used to say some people weren't made for this world, and Charlie was one of them. Danny said it too. I didn't remember much, if anything about the time before, but Charlie was twelve when things went to shit. He wasn't the Boy Scout that Danny was and he wasn't an engineer. Danny said, as a kid, Charlie wasn't particularly good or bad at anything. He just sort of slid through everything, mediocre at best and unreactive except to avoid the worst of things. He was terrible at planning and fighting and always had been. He was close to our mom, and when she died, he was lost. Danny thrived, and I had never known anything else, so we hadn't been much comfort to him. When Charlie lost his leg, he was done. I was outright annoyed by him, but at least while Danny was alive, he had been able to keep the peace between us. Now every day was me being pissed that he wasn't Danny and thinking the wrong brother died, something Charlie agreed with me about.

"Sara isn't really your sister, is she?"

"Are you asking if she's my mother's daughter?" I shrugged. "No. She isn't. We found her with a dead woman in a barn. But she's our sister, doesn't matter where she came from."

"Of course she is. I just meant she isn't blood related. You look nothing alike. How old were you? When you found her?"

"Fourteen."

"Old enough to be her mother," Claire said. We collected our stuff and set out.

"I guess. Family is family."

"Mothers are important," Claire said. She got a dark look on her face as she scrunched her brow. "Missing them is never good."

"Where's your family?" I asked.

"I have no family," she said grimly and with such finality that I knew better than to ask anything else.

We walked on in silence for an hour or so. As late

afternoon rolled around, we saw something in the distance. I spotted a fire. A group. I stopped and pointed.

"We're going past them. Don't make friends."

"Okay," she said, agreeing too casually with my directive for my taste. I expected more argument. That was more unsettling than the new people.

When we got closer, I could see that it was a family. They were in bad shape. They looked hungry and filthy. The mother was pregnant and there were three other small children, all younger than ten. The kids were skinny, and they sat in the dirt, staring idly at the sad, smoky campfire. The woman stirred something in a pot while the man sharpened a knife. He wasn't doing a great job with it. They'd starve in a month out here, but that wasn't my problem.

The sight bothered Claire. She stared sadly at the pregnant woman and little children. I nodded at the man and we eyed each other cautiously. They were as suspicious of us as we were of them. I kept my distance and moved slowly. I thought Claire was right behind me, but she wasn't. When I turned and looked, she was stopped and rummaging around in her pack. She pulled out all her food—canned goods and apples—and gave them to the woman.

"For you and your family," Claire said. She smiled at the children and handed them each an apple.

"Oh, we can't take it. You'll need it," the woman said.

"We'll manage," Claire said. "I hope you find somewhere safe soon."

"We're trying to find my sister in Piney Bottom. She left six months ago and told us things were better there than the First Circle."

"Claire, come on. Gotta go," I said.

"I hope you find her and I hope she is right," Claire said, smiling at the woman.

The woman motioned toward their fire. "It's late. You're welcome to share."

"Ah, no thanks," I said. "When it gets dark, put that fire out. Too many things get drawn in by the fire." I grabbed Claire's arm. "Come on."

Claire gave me a dirty look, but she started moving. The woman thanked us again while the children just stared at the apples, like they had no idea what to do with them. The father kept on with his knife. I didn't like it, not at all. I quickened our pace. "Are we going to stop?" Claire asked. Her voice had an icy, annoyed tone.

"Not for a while. I want distance between us and them."

"They were starving Emily."

"It appeared so, yes."

"Appeared? They were skin and bones. Those children were dying."

"Something wasn't right there. I told you to keep moving and follow my lead."

"I couldn't leave them without helping," she yelled.

"For fuck's sake, keep it down," I said, hushing her. "Maybe you helped them and maybe you didn't. No matter what, I doubt they make it to Piney Bottom. That fire will draw in all sorts of zeds and who knows what else, so either they don't have the slightest fucking clue as to how to make it out here or they know exactly what they're doing. Either way, I don't want any part of it."

"I-I didn't think—"

"Yeah, because you don't fucking know either, which is why I asked you to follow my lead." I sighed and started walking again. "Let's get some distance between us and them before we stop."

She nodded contritely and fell in line behind me. I walked another couple of miles before I called a stop. We made a fireless camp up against the riverbank where there was a hollow space. Nobody could see us except from the other side.

Up until that night, I hadn't heard any animals, no birds, nothing. That night we heard all kinds of night birds calling. I preferred silence, and tightened my grip on my knife. Claire was uneasy too. She shifted around nervously and backed up against the bank. I heard something moving toward us in the grass. I backed away from the embankment and toward the river. Whatever it was wasn't big, maybe a dog or coyote, but it was steady. When a form approached, it was small, but it wasn't a dog. One of the skinny, vacant-eyed kids from the camp stood on the bank and looked down at us. In the moonlight, I could see that he was covered in something shiny and black. In the light, I knew it wouldn't be black. It would be red.

Claire looked horrified. "What happened? Is he hurt?" She walked toward him and he simply stood still and stared at her.

"No! Claire, don't—" I said, but was cut off when something big tackled me from the side and the world went dark.

17

When I woke up, my arms were above my head, tied together around a horizontal pole that stretched between two trees. I blinked and shook my head to clear it. It throbbed. I'd been hit in the head enough to recognize the headache that was the result of somebody knocking you out. Claire was tied in the same way right next to me, and next to her was another girl. The girl cried and sobbed.

"This isn't good," Claire said. She looked at me carefully. "They hit you in the head. You were unconscious."

"I figured that out already." I looked around. Three filthy, scraggly tents around a fire made up the camp. The pregnant woman was busy doing chores. She was joined by another pregnant woman and the dirty little kids were milling about. The kids looked out of it as if they were drugged. They weren't though, they were just inbred or something. A third woman with long, stringy blonde hair came out of a tent. She pulled her dress straight and the man from the night before followed her out. She was the only one of the women not knocked up, but it appeared he was trying to change that. I scanned the surrounding area. They had taken us to the other side of the river.

I took a look at Claire. She looked fine except for being tied up. "Have you seen all of them?"

She nodded. "I think so. The family from last night. Two more women and one more man. He went off by himself a little while ago."

"Only two men?" I asked. They got the drop on me the night before. They wouldn't be so lucky again.

"I don't think the women are exactly pushovers," Claire said. "They seem meaner."

"Oh they probably are. I'm meaner." I checked out the other girl. "Hey. You. What's the story here?" I scooted closer to Claire and kicked the other girl when she didn't answer. "Hey. You hear me?"

She looked up, dazed. Her eyes were glazed over. She was on something.

"Shit. Claire, don't eat or drink anything here."

"Yes, *I* figured *that* out already," she rolled her eyes at me. "She's drugged. I think the children are drugged."

One of the little boys walked over to us and stared. His face was streaked with filth and he wore only a dirty pair of shorts. His eyes looked clear though, not like our fellow captive's.

"Nah. They're not drugged. They're just inbred little shits." I kicked at the kid and he scattered. "Fucking weirdos."

"They lay traps on the trail for people," Claire said.

"Yep."

"So what do they intend to do with us?" Claire asked.

The other girl laughed and sobbed. "Eat us."

"Yeah, they're definitely going to try and eat us," I said.

Claire looked horrified. "What?"

"Trapping a person is way easier than trapping game." I motioned to the camp. "They move around. Set up near different trails."

"They're sick," Claire said. She stared daggers at the man. He had wild bushy hair and a swarthy black beard that was unkempt. He stared back at her. "So what are we going to do?"

"Get the fuck out of here," I said. "I'm going to have to get free."

We looked at the pole. I pulled on it. It was solid aluminum, and it was chained to the two trees. We wouldn't be able to break free. The rope that bound us wasn't anything special, but it was well tied. I couldn't break it either. Our stuff was in a pile next to one of the tents. They'd rummaged through the packs and things were strewn about. The whole time, I hadn't heard any of them utter so much as a grunt at each other. The silence and their lack of communication were unnerving. Claire picked up on it too.

"I know they can speak, but they don't." She pointed to the women. "They don't say anything, but they do. It's unsettling."

"Yeah, they're freaks," I said. "Lots of people like them out here."

"I'm not sure they are people. At least the infected can't help themselves. These people are… sinister."

I agreed. "They are disgusting fucks."

"How are we going to stop them?" Claire asked.

"Stop them?" I looked at her and shook my head.

"We can't just leave them and allow them to keep doing this," she said.

"Umm, I don't know how you think I'm going to stop them. Other than gutting them all, I can't do anything." I motioned to the pregnant women and the kids. "You want me to kill them?"

"You can't kill them. But how do we stop them?"

"We don't. We get the fuck away as fast as possible."

"There has to be a way." Claire tried to relax, and I could tell she was thinking it through.

We stayed like that all day. Quietly observing the camp's routine. At mid-day, the second man came back. He looked exactly like the other one. Same beady eyes, same coloring and build. Same scraggly hair and swarthy look. I figured them to be brothers. The one that came back was fatter than his brother. He spent fifteen minutes chewing on a piece of jerky and staring at us. He stared at Claire the longest. The brother came over and joined him. He pointed at Claire.

"Keep her a while," he said.

The other nodded and finished his jerky. "Old one or that big un?"

He looked me over. I snarled at him. They hadn't tied my legs, which was a big mistake, and I had refused to eat or drink anything so I wasn't slow, like the other girl. The choice was easy. He pointed to the other girl.

"Her."

"Yep," the other brother said.

He went into one of the tents and came back with a small sledgehammer. He walked over to the girl calmly and used the hammer to brain her. The girl slumped immediately and began to convulse. Claire gasped. The blood hit her full on the face. She looked like she had no idea what just happened.

The man pulled out my knife and cut the dead girl loose from the pole. They stripped her and hung her up by her ankles from a tree. I knew what was coming next when he put the bucket under her head, but Claire didn't. She screamed when he slit the girl's throat and let her bleed into the bucket. She threw up when they gutted the girl and quartered her. They had her butchered in short order. The women took one of the girl's thighs, cut it up, and began cooking it. The children buzzed around excitedly as the meat sizzled over the fire. That was the first time I'd seen them look alive.

Claire was green with disgust. "They are animals," she whispered as she watched them eat. The brothers got served first, the kids last, but when the women gave the children meat, the weird little shits tore into it like runners tore into people. They growled and snarled and fought each other for every scrap.

"That's an insult to animals," I said.

When everyone had eaten their fill, they went to bed. All the little kids in one tent, and each brother to his own. One took two of the women and the other brother got the one who wasn't pregnant. I took advantage of the fact that we had to listen to them fucking in both tents and made a plan.

"Claire, you need to reach into my shirt and grab the pocket knife."

"You hid it in your bra?"

"Yes. Hold it tight. If you drop it, we're fucked." If she

dropped it, we wouldn't be able to pick it up because of the way our hands were tied.

I got close to her and maneuvered so that my chest was near her hands. She was steady and careful as she rummaged around.

"Ok. Got it. I'll hold it steady. You ease away."

"You're sure you're gripping it tightly?" I asked.

"Yes, Emily. I understand the dilemma. I have a good grasp of both the situation and the knife."

"Ok, for fuck's sake," I said as I moved slowly away from her. She had the knife. "Open it and hold the blade toward me. I'm going to cut the rope. Don't saw or anything. I'll do the work. You just hold it tight."

"Hurry up," she said.

The sounds of sex had quieted. At least while they were banging, we knew they were distracted. One of the kids coughed in their tent. We had to be quick. All it would take was for somebody to need to take a piss and we'd be done. I sawed the rope by moving my hands up and down against the knife blade. Claire's hands started to shake. I stopped a second, she reformed her grip, and we went back to it. It seemed like an eternity, but finally the rope broke. I rubbed my wrists, then I cut Claire free.

"You run straight back to the river. Get across it. I'm getting our stuff," I said.

"No, let's just go!" She grabbed my arm.

"We need that stuff." I folded the penknife and stuffed it back in my bra.

"I can't find the river on my own. If you're here, I'm here. Just hurry up."

I crept over to our stuff. The food was trashed, but they hadn't bothered the water bottles. I crammed as much stuff as I could into the packs. Our weapons were missing. I wanted them back. I looked around and found a nice rock. It was round and heavy but fit in one hand. Then I pulled a smoldering log from the fire pit. I put it right next to one of the tents. It began to melt the nylon, and the tent began to smolder then burn. I waited beside the tent opening. When the guy inside realized his tent was on fire, he came out, wild-eyed and naked. I brained him with the rock. It didn't drop him right away, so I jumped on him and bashed him a few more times until I was covered in his brains and blood. The woman came out screaming. It wasn't a fearful scream, it was an angry one. She flew at me and scratched and bit for all she was worth. I bit back. I threw her off me and brained her with the rock too. I wasn't sure she was dead and couldn't be, because by that time, the other brother had come out of his tent. He was naked as well and he had my knife.

When he saw his brother, he screamed with rage and came at me with the knife. He wasn't a fighter. He was just a mean piece of shit with a knife. He had no idea what to do with it. He slashed at me a few times and I easily avoided the blows. Finally, he launched himself at me and tackled me to the ground. He stabbed me in the shoulder before I could get a handle on him. I screamed in pain and rage myself. And I bucked. He went flying. I pulled the knife out of my shoulder and smiled at him. He scrambled to his feet and tried to charge me again but I sidestepped, and as he went by, I jammed my knife into his kidney and twisted. He fell to the ground, bleeding. I finished him off by slashing his throat. He choked and sputtered as he bled out.

The pregnant women and the dirty little kids stood still and stared at me. I was covered in blood. Claire had our packs.

"Emily, let's just go," she said gently.

I stared back at the women. They were as twisted as the men were and whatever came out of them would be just as sick. The little kids were unaffected to see me standing there all bloody after having just killed their fathers. They seemed bored and went back inside their tent. The women began to cry.

"You can save the tears," I said. "I'm leaving, but if I ever see either of you again, I'll kill you."

They nodded and went back inside the tent with the children.

I stared at the tent. I wanted to burn it and everything inside it. Those kids weren't human. Those women weren't human. But even I couldn't murder two pregnant women and a bunch of kids. Death would find this bunch soon enough.

Claire and I walked out of that camp, uneasy. The business felt unfinished, but sometimes things worked out that way. The situation was resolved even if it wasn't exactly satisfied and sometimes that was the best that we could do. We headed back toward the trail and didn't stop walking until well after dawn.

18

"Emily, stop. We need to take a look at your shoulder." Claire called the halt after the sun had risen. It was a nice, warm morning, with a slight breeze that rippled the tall grass around us. We made a left-hand turn at the river and followed it a ways instead of going right back out to the trail. The water gurgled and swirled. On the other side, I could see a few zeds milling around. They started to amble our way, but we were on the other side and they were no threat.

I sat down on the riverbank and pulled off my shirt while Claire fetched some water. She cleaned the knife wound and poked it.

"It's not bad. I wish I had the means to sew it up."

"It's fine. I've had way worse than that," I said. That was kind of a lie. I didn't recall ever getting stabbed, but

I'd been beaten up and slashed plenty of times. I could still move my arm. It hurt, but pain was a normal thing to live with.

Claire bandaged the wound tightly. "I'm glad you didn't kill them all," she said.

"You thought I would kill pregnant women and little kids?"

"I think you'll do whatever you have to do. I'm glad you didn't have to," she replied.

I should have. They deserved to die for the things they did, but then again, maybe so did I and so did everyone else who did questionable things to survive. I would have said luring travelers and eating them was kind of beyond questionable, but easy meat was easy meat, I guessed. I was just glad to be clear of them and back to finding Charlie and Sara.

"We can't afford much rest. We got well off the trail with that nonsense. We need to hurry now." I shouldered the pack and winced.

"I'm fine. Let's go," Claire said. She shouldered her own pack and started walking, but I could tell that she was tired. Her eyes were red, and she was clumsy when she walked.

"You sure? I guess we could stop for a couple of hours," I said.

"No. I'm ready. We can rest when we find your family." She never stopped walking.

"Alright," I said. I walked ahead of her, and we turned right so we could hit the trail. It took an hour or so to find it but when we did, I noticed that the trail wasn't fresh anymore. The horse crap and things in the road suggested that nobody had been through recently, as in not in a week, at least. I stood up after examining the trail and I weighed our options.

The old sign could have meant that we were way behind the caravan still, or that we were now ahead of them. I had a hard time choosing. We had been delayed, but we should still have been closer than a week. On the other hand, how had we gotten ahead of them? Had the cannibals taken us that far north and east so as to be in front? I looked at the hills and landmarks around. I had been to Piney Bottom plenty of times and we were no more than a day and a half from town.

"I'm not sure if we should go forward or back the trail," I said. I looked both directions for a sign. "I kind of think we're ahead of them now."

"How could that happen? We've been delayed several times," Claire said.

"Maybe they got delayed too. Weather, broken axel, zeds? I don't know what happened, but nobody has been on this trail for more than a week, and there is no way they were that far ahead."

"Ok, so we go back the way we came." Claire started back the trail.

I followed cautiously as I ran through all the possible dangers in my head and tried to decide if Charlie could handle any of them. My hope was that if he couldn't, Desmond, the Caravan boss, could. Des was a friend of Danny's. He wasn't a great guy, but he wouldn't hurt Charlie or Sara. At least not for free, and I had Clay pay him well to keep them safe. If he didn't hold up his end, he better hope I never found him, and he knew I would find him, eventually.

Sara knew basics. She knew weather stuff, camping stuff, how to handle shamblers, and how to avoid runners. She was more competent than Charlie was, but she was seven—just a kid, and kids got scared. I worried that something might have been more than any of them could handle.

We hadn't been walking long when I saw movement on the horizon and spotted horses. I started walking faster and passed Claire, who struggled to keep up with me. When we got to the travelers, I saw that it wasn't the caravan I expected. The big white draft horses stopped, and the driver cussed me for stopping them. He had his hand on a big club and he scowled at me.

"What'd you stop me for?" he growled.

"Easy, buddy. Is this Desmond Culvers' group?" I asked.

"No it ain't. Does it look like I'm running whores?" He pointed behind him, and I could see that it was cargo and families. Lots of kids and a distinct lack of women who looked like prostitutes.

"Well, I'm looking for him. You see him on the trail?"

"That sack of shit was behind us. Wanted to cut in front of me at the first stop, but something held them up."

"What was it?" I asked. I had a panicky feeling about that. Why would he want to cut ahead? It was safer to be behind this group for sure.

"I don't have any idea and I don't care. He owes me money and until he pays up, I ain't givin' a mouse fart's worth of help to him."

"So he is behind you?" Claire pointed back the trail. "Come on, let's go." She was clearly trying to distract me from the worry over the delay, but I stayed put.

"You have an extra horse? I'll bring it back to you in Piney Bottom."

He shook his head. "Girl, I don't know you. I ain't giving you no horse."

"You likely knew my brother, Daniel Wells," I said.

"Wells. Now I know why you looked familiar. Seen you fight once." He tightened his grip on his club. "Didn't know your brother and I ain't got any extra horses. You try and take one and see how that goes."

"I'm not a thief," I said as I stepped forward to him, angry at the insinuation. "I'm just trying to find my family. You could help, but I guess you don't want to. Fair enough, but I'll remember it."

"They weren't far behind us. Half a day at most," he said. "You won't need any horses to catch up to them."

"Whatever you say old man. You better hope you never need my help someday." I stalked back the trail with Claire following behind.

We passed four more wagons in the party. Two had food and supplies bound for Piney Bottom. The other four wagons had people, a lot of people. They were over-loaded, and the big draft horses strained in their traces to pull.

"Looks like people were really intent on leaving the city," Claire said. There were families with small children. I wasn't sure why you would risk being on the trail with babies. These people had to have been desperate. They were filthy and skinny; I knew that the passage on this caravan had cost them everything they had and maybe more.

They stared at us, and when they recognized me, the excited, hushed whispers started. Some of the older kids wanted to shake hands and chat. I got mired down in them for a bit, shaking hands and chatting. This group had left the city before I tossed biting zeds up into the crowd, so they didn't seem to be as afraid, but I was famous for killing, so they were friendly. When I said firmly that I had to go, they had sense enough to let me. I waved to them and trotted away.

Knowing we were barely a half day away made me go

faster. I jogged a bit and walked briskly in intervals. It was a good way to cover longer distances. Claire had fallen way behind. I could still see her, but she was almost a hundred yards behind me. I knew she would be fine as long as she had eye contact. I just couldn't stop for her.

There was a rise in the plain, and as I crested it and saw what had played out with the caravan, my heart stopped in my chest and I felt that strange prickly, slow feeling as the adrenaline coursed through me. The big lead wagon blocked the road; the huge black horses that pulled it were both dead. The two other wagons were pulled off the road on either side. Zeds were eating the corpses of the horses and mules. Traveler's bodies littered the trail. Along the side of the road, two crosses had been erected, and zeds tried to reach the men that hung from them. I pulled my knife and sprinted down the hill, desperately hoping that I wasn't going to find two familiar corpses among the piles.

19

My heart was pounding so hard when I got to the bottom of the hill that I was shaking and out of breath. I was used to fighting, but it was a lot easier to stay calm when I knew that Sara and Charlie were safe. In my mind, there was a little voice that always helped me in these situations right before a fight. It had always been Danny's voice I heard, telling me to slow down. Have a plan. Execute the plan. Stay calm. I stopped and listened. There it was, telling me all those things, but it wasn't Danny's voice I heard, it was Claire's. I paused a moment and caught my breath. I willed my heart to beat in a regular, normal rhythm as I looked at the area and assessed.

There was nothing to be done except to deal with all of the shamblers and look for Charlie and Sara. I couldn't look for them if I was worried about being bitten, so I pulled out my baton and got a good grip on my knife. There were four zeds calmly eating the horse at the head of the caravan. I brained them all as they were distracted. I stayed low and quiet as I checked under the wagon and inside. Nothing. All the gear was still there, and it hadn't been picked over.

I took out four more zeds between the lead wagon and the second one. They were easy enough to deal with if they didn't bunch up and come at you all at once, but as I got to the second wagon, my movement had attracted attention, and they started to form a bigger group. It was much more like fighting in the arena, so I didn't panic. I focused and got into the killing rhythm—swing, bash, stab, swing bash, stab. They growled and grabbed at me, but they were slow and I pushed them off easily as I dealt with each one. Fifteen lay still all around me. I headed over to the other wagon. It had been pushed over on its side and caved in. From the tracks all around, it looked like vehicles with heavy-duty tread tires had circled them and done the crashing. People were trapped beneath the wagon, but the zeds had gotten to them. After I cleared the shamblers out, I checked to see if Sara or Charlie were among them. They were not there.

The last group to deal with was the ones grabbing for the men hanging on the crosses. I stopped and calmed myself again. I counted twenty-five of them around both crosses. That was a lot, and I was tired, but I could see the men on the crosses were still alive. One of them was Desmond. I heard something behind me and whirled, ready to bash it, but it was Claire.

She was red-faced and out of breath but she had finally caught up. She had her baton out and ready. "You can't get them all on your own," she said.

"Oh, I could, but it's going to be easier with you here. I want you to make a lot of noise and draw them off a bit, get some separation. Keep moving, circle the crosses."

She was tired too, and this was not going to be easy for her, I knew, but she nodded and did exactly as I asked. She yelled and pounded the ground and waved her arms as she moved in a circle. It worked. The zeds began to peel off from the crosses and go for Claire. As they straggled off in pursuit, I weaved among them, stabbing and bashing until twenty-five corpses littered the area in a gory concentric circle.

Claire and I were both exhausted. She was bent over; hands on her knees, unable to catch her breath, and my arms shook as I willed myself to catch my breath. There had been a few close shaves when one got too close to Claire and when my knife stuck in a skull, but overall it had been simple.

I looked at the crosses. The man I didn't know was dead. When I cut him down, I didn't get a pulse at all. He had been stabbed several times in the stomach and bled out. Desmond was on the other cross and he was still alive. He moaned like a zed and cried when I cut him down. He was dying too. The wound in his stomach was more precise. It was in a good location to cause him a lot of pain but give him a slow death. Claire probed the wound gently and shook her head.

"Desmond, can you hear me?" I asked.

His eyes searched and found mine, and when he recognized me, he looked afraid.

"Wasn't my fault, Emily."

"It's okay, Des. What happened?"

He grimaced as Claire bound his stomach. "They hit us from behind. Trucks. Gathered everyone up. They were looking for them."

"Where are Charlie and Sara?" I asked.

"Took them. Set the zeds loose on everyone else." He coughed and moaned. "Big red-headed bitch. Stabbed Bobby and me. Hung us up. Wanted me to tell you it was her."

I nodded. I knew exactly who he was describing and in my gut was an even mixture of rage and fear. "Yeah. I know her."

Claire looked perplexed. "Rilla?"

"That's her," Desmond said. He grabbed my arm. "I swear I didn't give them up Emily."

"I know, Des," I said. "This isn't your fault. It's mine. I'm really sorry."

"Gotta go sometime, I guess. I'm glad I wasn't infected is all." He closed his eyes. "You do it for me?"

I nodded. "I will."

Claire put her hand on mine when I pulled out my knife. "What are you doing?"

"We can't take him with us. He'll die slowly. Not fun."

She looked sad. "I know you're right, but this just doesn't seem like—"

"I know. But it is the right thing to do," I said. "Thank you for trying Des."

"Your brother was a good friend, even though we didn't see eye to eye sometimes." He looked at me and smiled. "Saw you fight a few weeks ago. That scream shit you did? I feel bad for that big red-haired cunt when you find her."

I smiled back. "She won't like what I give her, I can promise you that," I said. "Ready?" I held my knife out.

"Nope, but go ahead anyway," he said.

I gave a couple of quick thrusts to the big blood vessel in his inner thigh. Blood bloomed rapidly, and he gripped my hand. It took longer than I thought it would, but after a few minutes, he was dead.

I stood up and looked back the trail, toward the city. "You should head back to the junkyard," I said. I pulled the key ring out of my bag and held it out to Claire. "You'll be safe there. Keep walking that direction," I said, pointing southeast. "Keep the sun on your left, and you'll hit the fence, eventually."

Claire shook her head no. "I'm going with you. You're going to exchange me for your family," she said.

I looked at her and laughed. "That's never going to work. They'll just kill all of us."

"What exactly is your plan Emily? You think you can just walk into the city and kill everyone in your path until you find Charlie and Sara?"

"That's exactly what I'm going to do," I said.

"That will never work. You need something to bargain with. That something is me."

"Claire, nobody wants you." I dumped everything but a couple small bottles of water from my pack and holstered the knife and baton.

"Commissioner Maynes does. Would she have sent Rilla for you? Do you really think you're that important? None of this was ever about you."

"And you think she sent this for you?" I laughed. "You're delusional."

"She wants what I know, and she wants me gone. She knows I'm safer out here with you and she knows how to get you to deliver me."

"Safer out here with me? That's stupid. Nobody is safe out here."

"I am one hundred percent safer out here with you than I ever was in the city."

"Claire, there are a million ways to die out here."

Claire smiled and nodded. "Yes, but you know how to handle most of them. She won't leave it to chance."

"Why does she want you?"

"I told you the first day. Because I can cure the infected. I threaten everything she's built. She needs this world. She wants this world and she'll do whatever she has to in order maintain it."

"That sounds every bit as crazy now as it did that first day I met you," I said. "I have to move fast, Claire. I don't have time for this."

"Wrong. They are not going to hurt them. If it was just about hurting you, they would have killed them and left them for you to find. Charlie and Sara are bait."

"So we'd be walking into a trap? What kind of plan is that?"

"Like I said, you're going to use me to bargain."

"What if they won't deal?" I didn't like anything about this plan. I didn't believe her at all, but she was right about Charlie and Sara. They wanted one of us back for sure or Charlie and Sara would be dead on the trail.

"I'll handle the negotiations. They'll be amenable." Claire said.

"You're nuts," I said.

"If I were, this would be so much easier," Claire said. She shouldered her pack. "Let's go. No matter what, I'm not leaving you now, so you might as well start walking."

"I could leave you in the dust now."

She laughed as she walked briskly back the trail toward the city. "You keep saying that, and yet here we are."

I wouldn't leave her. At least not on the trail alone. I would figure out something else. I had plenty of time to think as we walked.

20

The trail was clear. Unnervingly clear, actually. No people, no zeds. It was as if our path had been deliberately made safe. We made fast time with the easy walk, and when we passed the place where the horde had come through, it was apparent from the trodden grass and trail marks that we were close to the city.

My plan was to pause at the forest. If we camped there for the night, I was sure I could sneak off and leave Claire. I didn't want to do it, but my plan, shitty plan such as it was, was to sneak back in to the city and find a way to get Charlie and Sara out. It wasn't well thought out at all, but I had no idea what else to do. My brother had one leg and my sister was seven. Even if I got in, getting out a crippled guy and a kid wasn't going to be easy.

The other part of the plan, the part where I ditched Claire and hoped she had learned enough to stay alive until I got back was equally as bad. I'd have to tie her up to stop her and that would leave her vulnerable. I knew my best hope there was to lose her in the trees. They were hard to navigate through and she sucked at it, anyway. She'd never keep up if I didn't want her to. But that also meant she'd be lost in the forest and vulnerable to people and zeds. Zeds she could probably handle, but people were a different thing entirely.

We walked in almost total silence the whole way; our conversation was limited to basic instructions. I knew that she was thinking of a way to get me to do what she wanted, and I was thinking of how to ditch her. We both knew a reckoning was coming, but we were unprepared for what it was when it finally came.

Any hope I had of losing her in the trees was gone. When we got to the place where the trees had been, all that was there was black, burned scrub. The fires we set to distract the herd had gotten bigger and consumed the whole forest. There was no place to leave her now. I stood and stared angrily at the charred earth. Claire looked at me, and she knew what I had been planning to do.

"Emily, it's my plan or nothing."

I nodded, but only because I couldn't think of anything else to do but agree with her. I started walking again, skirting the black circle where the trees had been. I stopped when I saw what awaited us at the gate to the First Circle.

Maynes' assistant, the little man in the neatly pressed grey suit, David Evans, waited patiently with a sizable host of guards. Rilla was with them. She looked very pleased with her new station in life as she grinned at me and played with a sword. Sara and Charlie were bound tightly to the gate. Both had hoods over their heads. They struggled against their bonds.

"Miss Wells, welcome home. I'm delighted to see you in such good health," Evans said when I stopped in front of them. The guards looked ready, but they made no move yet. They all had cattle prods and batons and there was thirty of them. Impossible odds. Even for me.

"David. Stop this. Let Emily and her family go. I'll go quietly," Claire said.

"Claire. Lovely to see you again as well," he said.

"I don't know what's going on, but let my family go and you can do whatever you want with me. Just make sure they're safe," I said.

"I think the time for that has passed Miss Wells." Evans nodded at Rilla, who walked over to Sara and Charlie. She pulled the hood from Sara's head. Sara blinked at the light but when she saw Rilla, she struggled angrily for all she was worth. She kicked at her and screamed around her gag.

"Sara, stop," I yelled. When I did, she stopped and saw me. Her eyes were wide, and she yelled for me. I smiled at her. "Everything is going to be fine. Just settle down." She nodded, and I saw the complete trust in her eyes. Everything was not going to be fine. Not even a little bit. I knew it by the hopeless sinking feeling I had in the pit of my stomach.

Rilla pulled the hood from over Charlie's head and when she did, Sara screamed against her gag and I heard Claire gasp beside me.

She cut the gag from his mouth and when she did, he let out a string of angry howls and started spitting at her. She laughed as she removed his leg and flung it aside, then cut him loose and let him fall over onto the ground. She grabbed his good leg and slung him out in the dirt between us. Charlie screamed and clawed at the ground as he tried to focus on someone to rip apart, only he flopped around and kept falling over, unable to figure out how to move in any one direction without his leg. The guards all laughed. They thought it was funny, I guess, watching him flop around like he did in a handicapped fit of rage. Rilla took a bow and stepped back in line.

I stared at her for a second or two as I let the rage boil. I imagined ripping her into pieces right there and I knew I could do it if there had been less of them or if I hadn't had Sara to consider.

I heard Charlie growl close by and saw he had settled

on Claire for a target. He had finally adopted a clawing, pull-crawl motion and was almost to her. I broke eye contact with Rilla and pulled Charlie back to me by his good leg. His eyes focused on me then and he came for me, faster and more agile than I had ever seen him move in life. I avoided his grasp and calmly sat down on his back, pinning him to the ground. He screamed and struggled against me and I smelled the sickness on him--that smell I'd smelled hundreds of times before when I'd killed runners, the mix of shit and vomit and rot.

None of this had been his fault, not any of it. He was likely always meant for this fate, but I had hoped that I could have spared him the experience, just like I knew that he had hoped he could have spared me the experience of putting another brother out of his misery.

I hadn't cried when I'd had to kill Danny. I knew I should have, but at the time, I had been overwhelmed with it. I had only been a sixteen-year-old kid myself. I hadn't flinched when I hit Danny and shoved a knife in his brain to keep him from coming back. I didn't flinch this time either when I pulled Charlie's snapping head back and cut his throat, but I did cry. I cried silent tears of sadness and rage, and I held him while he bled to death. When he stopped moving, I shoved my knife into the base of his skull and twisted it so he could finally be at peace.

I pulled my knife free and walked over to David

Evans. I stood there for a second and stared at him. The guards moved closer but Evans stopped them. He smirked at me even as I cleaned my brother's blood off on his neatly pressed suit. I stepped back, dropped the knife at his feet, and waited.

The blow I expected never came.

"Kindly escort Miss Wells and Miss Maynes to their cell," he said.

21

The door to my cell closed and locked for the first time since I'd been a fighter. Nobody had ever bothered to do it before, as I was a volunteer, but now I was most definitely not there voluntarily, so Vance had to lock the door.

He looked sad and apologetic. "I'm really sorry Em, but—"

"It's ok Vance. I'm probably safer this way anyway," I said. The other cons had screamed and catcalled at us when they brought us in. If they let us out into the general areas, I would be in a constant fistfight. It would have made me happy, actually. I was ready to kick the shit out of someone. Any of them would do.

He nodded. "Watch your back in the yard. I'll do what I can," he whispered.

"You're a good guy. I appreciate it, but don't do anything dumb to get yourself in trouble on my account," I said.

"Well, I figure, we all look out for one another, maybe we make things better." He motioned toward Claire, who was sitting on her bunk, looking pissed.

"Or you get yourself locked up. Just be careful. I'll be fine." I sat down on my own rack and tried to relax. It was impossible. They took Sara, and I wasn't about to let her stay in an orphanage or wherever they took her.

"They won't hurt her, at least not yet," Claire said. She knew what I had been thinking.

"I don't trust that assessment."

"They won't. She is insurance that you will behave and do what they want," Claire said.

"I don't think they're worried. I'm locked up," I said.

Claire gave a small laugh. "You can still give them trouble. Anyone who knows you at all knows that." She stopped laughing and got serious. "The Commissioner will offer you a deal, and Emily, you have to promise me that you'll take it."

"I won't promise that. Who is she to you?" I had wanted to ask but for some reason, I was afraid to hear the answer.

"My mother."

I couldn't believe I hadn't figured it out. They looked alike—same eyes, nose, lips—but there was a cruelty in the Commissioner that Claire just didn't possess. Still, other than build—the commissioner was taller—they looked almost exactly alike.

"Your own mother put you in here?" I couldn't fathom what it would take for a mother to do that. My mom died when I was eight, but she had been kind, gentle, and had given her life for us. It was completely foreign to me that any mother wouldn't do the same.

"She did," Claire said grimly.

"How is that, I mean, how could she do that?"

"She puts this place, this thing she's built here, above everything."

"How are you threatening this shitty city?"

"I told you, I can cure the infected. It will change everything. Some people don't want anything to change. You don't remember what it was like before, but I do. Many do, and many want to move on. My mother is not one of them."

"So, say you don't have it. Lie."

"I won't. I can help people. I won't stop trying." Claire shrugged. "Besides, she has seen it work."

"Claire, you can't help anyone if you're dead."

"It's too late for any of that. Listen to her offer Emily."

"I don't care what she offers. She killed my brother. She'll pay for that."

Vance and another handler appeared at the door.

Vance held out a pair of handcuffs apologetically. The other guy grinned and whacked the bars with his baton.

"Let's go Wells."

"Go where?" I stayed on my rack and didn't even look at him.

"The days of you being Queen Bee are over. Get the fuck over here and put the cuffs on before I come in there and put them on you." He whacked the bars again.

"Come on in here and try it," I said. I turned my head to face him and stared. His face got red, and he sputtered.

"Please, Emily?" Vance said. "Somebody wants to see you."

I smiled sweetly at Vance. "Sure thing," I stood up and took the cuffs from Vance and cuffed myself. "All you had to do was ask nicely."

"Emily don't antagonize them," Claire said. "Listen to the offer."

I shrugged and tried to look bored as they led me out to one of the decontamination rooms. They made me sit crossed-legged and cuffed my ankle to a ring in the floor, then cuffed my hands to the ring as well. It was almost as bad as being hog-tied. I could barely move, and I couldn't do much, if any, damage from the position.

"Somebody must be really scared of me, huh?" I said, making a kissing noise at the guard. He backhanded me, and I glared at him. He and Vance left me, and I sat there for a bit. I knew perfectly well who wanted a word with me.

My theory was confirmed when Maynes glided through the door. Her perfectly pressed, white shirt gleamed in comparison with the dull grey room. She stood in front of me and looked relaxed as she smiled down at me. "Well, that seems extreme," she said, motioning to my restraints.

"Really? Because I don't think they are extreme at all," I replied, glaring at her.

"Emily, I deeply sorry about what happened to Charlie. My people told me that it happened on the way back. It was a tragic accident, but one you full well know is a rather common occurrence when people choose to travel."

"Save your lies. What do you want?"

"I want for things to be well between us again." She knelt and gave me a concerned look.

"Never gonna happen. Is that all?"

"Well, it could happen, actually. What if I said I would be happy to let you free? Sara too. Set you up inside the Fifth Circle. You know, in Ancient Roman times, great gladiators could retire, and they were loved and well respected."

"I wouldn't live within twenty miles of you." I spat at her feet. She didn't move, but her eyes went from false concern to cold hatred. In a flash it was gone, and she gave me the concerned look again.

"Think of Sara. She's only seven years old. Don't you want her to be safe and well cared for? She could go to school. Neither of you will ever want for anything."

I just stared at her, so she went on.

"Or you may choose to leave. Go to a different settlement. We'll get you safe passage anywhere you like." I said nothing, and she smiled a mirthless smile. I figured it was the only kind of smile she was capable of smiling. "On Sunday, you will have one final match. You and Claire, together. When you open the box, there will be a sword in it. Kill Claire and I'll let you and Sara go free. Do anything else and you won't like what happens."

"How do I know you won't kill me, anyway?" I asked.

"I suppose you don't, but I swear to you, if you don't kill her, you will all die." She knelt down to my face and looked me squarely in the eye. "Do you believe me?"

I didn't flinch. "Your own daughter?"

She kept the same expression, but her eyes were black and cold and dead. "I do whatever is necessary to protect people. We're alike, you and I."

"We're nothing alike. You killed my brother. I'm going to take the same knife I used to put him out of his misery and I'm going to shove it in your skull. I promise."

"Kill Claire, or the last thing you will see, Miss Wells, before somebody shoves a knife in *your* skull, will be your seven-year-old sister being eaten alive." She stood up and smiled. "*I* promise."

She left me there, thinking of all the ways I could kill her and how much I would enjoy every single one of them. When Vance and the other idiot came to retrieve me, I went quietly. I didn't say anything as I climbed into my rack and stretched out.

"She wants you to kill me, doesn't she?"

"I never saw anyone. They were just harassing me," I said.

"You're a great fighter Emily, which is a good thing, because you are a terrible liar," she said.

22

We waited in the ready room while the fights went on in the Arena. Of course, we were the last fight of the day—the main event. I waited for them to do something crazy, tie us together like last time, but they didn't. We were the last people in the room. Claire was oddly calm. I guess she figured she was about to die no matter what, so why freak out? She stood still and ready. She breathed deeply and calmly, and she didn't fidget, didn't push her glasses up like she normally did.

I, on the other hand, paced from one end of the room to the other. I'd asked several times that week to see Sara, but they wouldn't let me. I didn't trust Maynes at all, but Claire had been right about the deal, so I knew she was probably right about Sara being safe until after the fight. I didn't know what to do. I was one hundred percent sure that we were about to die. No way was Maynes going to take any chances. The odds would be terrible—likely all runners—and even with a good sword, we'd be in trouble.

But did I trust her to keep her word if I killed Claire? I had a funny feeling in the pit of my stomach that I could, and that really bothered me. Had it just been me, I would have gone out fighting. I had never hoped for much better when I volunteered. But it wasn't just about me. It was about Sara. If there was even a small chance that she could be safe, I should take it, no matter what I had to do. Claire didn't disagree. She'd been yammering at me all week about it. I refused to acknowledge there was a deal, let alone debate ends justifying means with her, but sometimes the end *did* justify the means, especially when Sara's life was at stake.

"Emily, stop pacing," Claire said. "You're making me nervous."

I glared at her, but I stopped. She laughed at me. I was about to retort when the door that led back to the dormitory swung open and a familiar figure entered.

"Hey kid," Clay said.

"Clay," I said as I nodded. He looked a bit rough, like somebody had beaten him up. I had a fairly good idea who, because she stepped in the room after him, along with three of her new gang. "I see you brought a bag of shit with you."

"How'd you like to fight your last fight with a broken arm?" Rilla asked.

"If you coulda, you woulda," I said. "You had plenty of opportunity all week to jump me. You're either too chicken or somebody is holding your leash tight."

She kept silent, and I knew I was right. Maynes wanted me whole and able to do what she wanted, or Rilla would have shanked me my first night back.

"Emily, I came to remind you of Maynes' offer. It's legit," Clay said.

"She sent you because she thought I would listen to you?" I laughed. "She clearly hasn't been paying attention."

"This is no joke Emily," Clay said. He held out his hands to me, pleading. "Sara is fine. She'll stay fine if you do as Maynes asks."

"I think you may as well say it, Clay. Emily has to kill me," Claire said.

"I don't like it, kid, but for once in your life, do something in your best interest." Clay touched my arm. "You can make it out of this."

I stared at him and smiled. "Sure, I can." I held out my hand to him. "Thanks for everything Clay. I know you didn't sell me out."

His face flushed. "I swear, I didn't."

"I know." I shook his hand firmly. "Take care of yourself. You're good at it."

"I was only trying to help you."

"I know."

"But it was my idea," Rilla piped up. "Got me out of the life. Great job now. I get to do basically whatever I want." She pulled out my knife, the big one I had dropped in front of Evans, and she shoved it into Clay's neck.

He made a few little mewing sounds like a kitten as he bled out. I held him as he died, and I was sorry. He had done what he thought best for me because he knew that I seldom, if ever, did what was best for me. I knew he was the one who gave up the plan because he was the only one who could. Rilla just tagged along. I patted his hand. "It's okay. I'll take care of everything."

"Yeah, I wanted to kill your girlfriend, said I'd be happy to gut her," Rilla said, "but her mommy said you had to be the one—"

I slammed my forearm into her nose, and when she dropped the knife, I gave her an uppercut that sent her flying. The other two came for me and I took them out with a well-placed stab to leg and kidney. Rilla screamed and came at me and I stepped into her, driving the knife into her gut and twisting it. She fell to her knees and stared at the wound then at me.

"You should have gutted us both when you walked in, but you had to strut around and explain how bad you are.

Moron. That was for my brother." I walked around behind her and pulled her head back, then I slit her throat and smiled as I watched her die.

I cut the other two's throats for good measure, cleaned the knife, and handed it to Claire. "Hide it. You might need it."

"If you don't kill me, you are an idiot," she said. She hid the knife in her waistband.

"We'll see," I said as the doors opened and we stepped out into the arena for the final time.

23

The mob was in their glory. They had gorged on a full day of carnage, and they sensed they were about to see something epic. They screamed and beat on the floors and area so much that it felt like the air was vibrating. I looked at Claire and nodded, then I stalked to the middle of the arena where the chest sat. I opened it, and true to her word, Maynes had provided a beautiful sword. It was light and perfectly balanced Damascus steel, gleaming and razor sharp. It was everything I could have ever wanted in a pull, the best thing I had ever seen, but today, it was the last thing I wanted to see.

I pulled the blade free and slammed the lid closed. I twirled it a few times and listened as the mob went nuts, screaming and pounding even harder.

"Do it fast," Claire said.

I could. I could kill her so fast and so cleanly that she wouldn't feel a thing. It would be an act of love and kindness, not one of violence. I'd done the same for both of my brothers, my family. It wouldn't be any different for Claire. I could have done it and ensured Sara's safety.

"It's okay, Emily. Please. Just do it," She smiled at me.

I ignored her.

I looked up into the stands and found Maynes in her box. She smirked at me and saluted, then pointed to the end of the arena. I looked down to the end, expecting to see a dozen runners come out of the chute. I would have been less panicked had that been the case. Sara came out of the chute, looking confused and terrified.

"Sara," I screamed as I dropped the sword and took off, sprinting to get to her.

She was holding back tears, but when she saw me, she ran as fast her legs could carry her, straight for me, then jumped into my arms. I hugged her tight and looked around. Nothing else yet. I carried her back to the middle, then I put her down and picked up the sword. I looked up into the Commissioner's box. Maynes smiled and nodded. She held out her hands in a gesture that said, ... *make your choice.*

"Emily, do it. Please. It's the only way," Claire said. She was crying. Sara frowned, walked over to her, and took her hand.

"It's okay. Em and me won't let anything get you," she said. She looked up at me and looked serious. "Right, Em?"

I smiled at her and nodded. "Right," I said, then I walked to Claire's other side, took her hand, and held it in the air. The mob went insane. I looked up into the stands. Maynes was smiling. I knew then that she knew exactly what I would do, and that no matter what, Sara and I would never have been safe. I dropped Claire's hand and saluted Maynes, then I gripped the sword and stepped out in front of Claire and Sara.

"You guys stay behind me. If they're runners, I'm going to disable them. Claire, use your knife and finish them off."

"We're going to have to get out of here," Claire said. She pulled the knife out of her waistband and got ready to fight.

"Yeah, well, we'll try and get to the fighter's box. If I say run, you guys go for it. Sara, you hear me? You run and don't look back." I pointed to the fighter's box, but when I did, I saw a line of handlers with cattle prods lining the wall. We weren't getting out that way. "Okay, scrap that plan."

"Em, what about the pens?" Claire asked.

"They're at the end, but—" I stopped and grinned at her. "That might work."

She nodded. "They won't be expecting that."

"Nope, they sure as fuck will not," I said. "Alright, see those big doors?" I pointed to the far side of the arena. "Go stand right next to them." There were two large, heavy wooden doors that swung open outward but from opposite directions. The Zed Pens. One for runners and one for shamblers. I didn't know what would come out of either door—they switched them up every time—but it didn't matter. Those pens would lead out eventually and that was the way we were going.

Sara and Claire ran down and stood between those doors. I stood back a bit, ready to take out whatever came out long enough to get them through.

"I'll go first and clear a path. No matter what, keep moving. Get through the door."

They both nodded and waited.

It was the door on the left. It opened slowly, creaking as it did, and when the space was just big enough, a runner came screaming out. The door opened all the way, and they poured out. I was the first thing they saw, they ignored Claire and Sara, and I had an idea.

"All of them! I got them. Get Sara inside and close that door!" I started yelling at the runners—fifteen of them— and I took off running to the other end of the arena. I sprinted, and I could still feel them behind me, running with all the infectious rage they had. I ran out of room when I hit the wall at the other end, but it had worked, they all followed me. I whirled and sliced the first one almost in half with the sword. It went through him like he was butter and pulled free clean and easy.

It was glorious.

I slashed and hacked, sending limbs flying in every direction. I had never had such a great blade. Light and sharp, it was like an extension of my arm, and even with them growling and spitting and lunging all over the place, I danced through them with that sword, ending their miserable infected lives, fueled by as much rage as any of them. I snarled and growled just like them as I killed all fifteen, and when I was done, I stood in the middle of the arena among the severed arms and bloody corpses, covered in gore, and I screamed. I screamed the same scream of rage and hatred I screamed during the match right before Claire.

I looked up and saw Maynes. She wasn't smiling. She looked flabbergasted and angry. I pointed to her with my sword and I screamed again, then I smiled at her and stalked toward the wall. I meant to climb up there and open her chest with my sword. I stopped when I heard the big door open again and a herd of shamblers poured out.

The mob screamed excitedly again, sensing that I was about to die. There were just too many of them. I'd been in situations with bad odds before, but this was beyond bad. I stopped counting at forty but there had to be half as many more. I couldn't take them all.

That was when I saw Claire's head poke out of the other door. She saw the herd and motioned me with her arm. I smiled and nodded. I didn't have to kill them all. I just had to get to the door.

I ran around the edge of them as they shambled out into the arena. When I got to the other end, I cut a path through them to the door. They bunched up and grabbed for me, but I slashed and took off arms and heads as I found them. They had all doubled back around with the commotion and the weird flocking sense they all seemed to have and converged on me and the door again. The door opened just a crack and Claire poked out again. She shoved the knife into a zed skull and pulled it out.

"Get in here!" She pushed it open a bit more and killed another one. I started back to her again, then I saw Sara poke her head out. She was looking for me, scared and crying. I went faster, and I was almost there when one of them came for her. I screamed and launched myself at it.

It got me on the forearm. It bit down hard and shook its head slowly, like a dog. Claire's knife came down into its skull and it flopped off me. "Let's go!" she said, and we scrambled through the door and closed it behind us.

I looked down at my mangled arm. The zed had taken a big bite. It was ragged, and blood oozed and welled in the hole. "Fuck," I said as I stared at it. I knew what that meant. I'd seen it three times before. My dad lasted twelve hours. My mom a day. Danny had lingered for two. I'd be lucky to get that. Maybe just enough to get Claire and Sara out of the city. I had to make it that long.

Claire ripped off a part of her shirt and bandaged the bite quickly. "You're going to be fine," she said. She looked over at Sara, who was hysterical. She hugged Sara. "Sara. It's okay. Em is going to be fine. We're going to get out of here and everything is going to be fine. I promise. Right, Em?"

I stood up and hugged them both. "That's right. Everything is going to be fine. So, stop crying and let's get out of here."

"You got bit," Sara sobbed.

"This?" I laughed. "That's nothing. Just a scratch. I'm going to be fine." I tousled her hair. "I promise." I hugged her and looked at Claire. I stopped smiling. She didn't say anything, but I could tell she was thinking. Her brow was furrowed, and she nodded.

We went for the outer door. It was locked. I screamed and kicked it, pounded it a couple of times, but it didn't budge.

I sat down in the dirt and laughed and cried.

I held the sword out the Claire. "Do it. Do it now before I turn."

"I won't. It won't come to that," she said.

"That's all it can come to," I said. "You know how this works."

She nodded. "I do. And know it won't come to that."

I jumped when the door opened. Vance stuck his head in and his eyes searched the room. When he saw me, he smiled a relieved smile and opened the door the rest of the way.

"He was the one opening them," Claire said.

I stood up and walked over to him. He grinned. "Emily, I—"

He shut up when I grabbed his face and kissed him. When I let him go, he was beet red and confused looking.

"I owe you everything," I said.

"I-I just wanted to help," he stammered.

"Medical," Claire said, rolling her eyes at him as she brushed by. "We need to stop by there."

"Two doors down and on the way," Vance said.

"Won't they be looking for us?" I asked.

"Not now. I let the main zed pen loose on the other side." He smiled. "We have time."

"Not much," I said, "but we'll make it enough." I grabbed my sword. "Let's go."

"What are you getting in medical?" I asked as we walked quickly down the hall. "You can't help me."

"You have your weapon, Emily. I have mine. Just trust me," she said.

She ducked inside quickly, and we waited outside. I heard a scuffle, and when it quieted, Claire emerged, looking angry and tousled, but she had a bag.

"Let's go," she said.

Vance led us out, and the path was clear. He opened the door and held it for us. It spit us out into an alley. "That's the Second Circle," he said. "If you can get to the First, you can maybe hole up there for a while." He looked down at my arm.

I hugged him. "Come with us," I said.

"No. I can't. I have to get back to my family." He smiled down at Sara. "Take care of Emily."

Sara nodded seriously and put her hand in mine. "I will." She pulled my hand. "Come on Em, we gotta go."

I hugged him one last time. "I won't forget what you did for us."

"You'd have done the same," he said.

"I would," I agreed. We left him and headed down the alley and out into the Second Circle. We stuck to the darkest spots we could, more alleys, and found rags to cover me up. I was starting to get dizzy and sweaty. My arm throbbed, and I imagined the poison from the zed spreading with every pulse. The world started to spin, and I realized that I had hours and not days.

I stopped. "Claire," I said, wobbling as I struggled to stay upright.

She turned and looked at me. Her face was profoundly serious, but not panicked. She grabbed me before I fell and leaned me against the wall of the alley. "I thought we could get a little further, but we'll just have to deal with this here." She put her hand on my forehead and nodded.

"I want to you to kill me now," I said. "Don't let Sara see me turn. Don't let me hurt anyone."

She rummaged around in her bag and pulled out a big hypodermic needle. "If it comes to that, I'll do it, but it won't."

"It will," I said. I began to shiver. I was freezing, and I couldn't stop shaking. "It always comes to this. Can you take care of Sara?"

"Of course, but I won't have to. You're going to be fine."

Sara cried and hovered behind her. I held out my hand to her, and she tackled me. "Don't be sick," she pleaded. "Please don't be sick."

"Listen, you're going to have to help Claire out, got it? Don't give her a bunch of grief," I said. She sobbed into my chest and I kissed her head. I ruffled her curly brown hair. "I love you so much." I cried too, and I hugged her as tight as I could.

"Emily, turn over onto your side," Claire said. She had used the syringe and drawn some blood from her arm.

"What the hell are you doing? Just kill me and get Sara out of here."

"You know your business. I know mine." She had another needle, a long one attached to a thin tube. "Roll over. Please."

She finally just shoved me over.

"I'm afraid this is going to hurt. A lot," she said.

"What is—"

I screamed. I couldn't see what it was exactly, but it was like a stabbing fire in my back. I felt a slight pressure. Claire pulled me over on to my back.

"Now we wait." She looked around the alley.

"Kill me," I said. "Please." I grabbed her hand and squeezed it. "I don't want to hurt you."

"You won't." She smiled. "But you're going to be sick for a while. No way around this part. Just close your eyes and rest. We'll be here when you wake up."

The world throbbed and swirled. Everything seemed far away, tiny, and yet gigantic and close all at the same time as the fever dug its heels in. I tried to form words but couldn't, and my eyes felt heavy and hot. In my mind, I begged her to take her knife and shove it through my temple, but Claire just smiled and held my hand. Sara held the other one. As I closed my eyes, I hoped one of them had the sense to kill me before I woke up.

24

When I opened my eyes, I was shocked and bewildered to be alive. I blinked a few times and adjusted to the harsh light. It felt like somebody was stabbing me in the eyes with needles. I closed them again and moaned. A small form shifted beside me and cuddled closer.

"It's okay. You'll be light sensitive for a while," Claire said.

I opened my eyes again and focused on her voice. "What happened?"

"You were infected. You had to ride it out."

I tried to sit up but couldn't. I was too weak, and none of my muscles felt like they would obey me, anyway. "How am I alive?"

"I have the cure," Claire said, "Or rather, am the cure. I inoculated you, but you still had to get sick. You're lucky you were so strong. Some don't survive the infection."

"I-I didn't turn?"

She shook her head. "No. You were out of it for a few days, but your fever broke last night. You'll be weak, but you'll live."

Sara hugged me tight. "I helped. We got water and food and Claire says we're going to go find her friends up North as soon as you're well."

"You couldn't possibly have friends," I said to Claire as I hugged Sara back. "That's the least believable thing you've ever said."

Claire laughed. "If you're insulting me, then we know you're going to be fine."

I looked around the alley. Rags and trash littered the ground, but they had made a comfortable bed for me. Families gathered in their alcoves. I recognized the alley. The same old woman who had helped us when we escaped sat next to Sara.

I looked up at Claire and smiled, then I closed my eyes and reclined. "I guess you're not as useless as I first thought. I did the right thing when I didn't let them beat you to death."

"You're much more pleasant unconscious," she said as she settled in next to me.

I hugged them both against me. We weren't out of the woods yet. We still had to get out of the city, but for the first time in a long time, I felt safe, and I felt like I could see a future worth fighting for.

ACKNOWLEDGMENTS

Books are hard to make. I mean, there are words, lots of them, and they have to be spelled correctly and used properly. Don't even get me started on the commas.

Anyway, I didn't do this alone. Thanks to my buddies Tom and Stefan from my original critique group, Hot Soup. They read the beginning of this story and after I finished, they gave helpful feedback. Thank you both.

Thanks to my other beta readers, Carrie and Tara. Thank you for reading and giving honest feedback.

Lastly, thanks to Jae. I could write an entire chapter on all the ways you have helped me. Thank you for your mad editing skills, your feedback, your support every single day, and just being you. Writing, working on projects with you, and hanging out are my favorite things. Ever. Everything is better with you. All the corn, always.

ABOUT THE AUTHOR

Jessica Raney is an author of speculative fiction. She has two collections of short stories: *Oddballs: A Collection of Short Fiction* and *Dreadful Pennies: A Collection of Short Things*. Her first full length novel, Tooth and Nail, was released in 2018. Her work has also appeared in the anthology, *Hair Raising Tales of Horror.* When not navigating Houston traffic or writing, she's dealing with her cat/dog/demon/baby, Gimli.

ALSO BY JESSICA RANEY

Oddballs

Dreadful Pennies

Tooth and Nail